"RIGHT IN FRONT OF YE," SHE ANSWERED, TURNING
QUICKLY.

THE NOVELS, STORIES
AND SKETCHES OF
F. HOPKINSON SMITH

TOM GROGAN

CHARLES SCRIBNER'S
SONS ❧ NEW YORK ❧ 1902

CONTENTS

vii

CONTENTS

ILLUSTRATIONS

FROM DRAWINGS BY GEORGE WRIGHT

TOM GROGAN

TOM GROGAN

I

BABCOCK'S DISCOVERY

SOMETHING worried Babcock. One could see that from the impatient gesture with which he turned away from the ferry window on learning he had half an hour to wait. He paced the slip with hands deep in his pockets, his head on his chest. Every now and then he stopped, snapped open his watch and shut it again quickly, as if to hurry the lagging minutes.

For the first time in years Tom Grogan, who had always unloaded his boats, had failed him. A scow loaded with stone for the sea wall that Babcock was building for the Lighthouse Department had lain three days at the government dock without a bucket having been swung across her decks. His foreman had just reported that there was not enough material to last the concrete-mixers two hours. If Grogan did not begin work at once, the divers must come up.

3

Heretofore to turn over to Grogan the unloading of material for any submarine work had been like feeding grist to a mill, — so many tons of concrete stone loaded on the scows by the stone-crushing company had meant that exact amount delivered by Grogan on Babcock's mixing platforms twenty-four hours after arrival, ready for the divers below. This was the way Grogan had worked, and he had required no watching.

Babcock's impatience did not cease even when he took his seat on the upper deck of the ferry-boat and caught the welcome sound of the paddles sweeping back to the landing at St. George. He thought of his men standing idle, and of the heavy penalties which would be inflicted by the government if the winter caught him before the section of wall was complete. It was no way to serve a man, he kept repeating to himself, leaving his gangs idle, now when the good weather might soon be over and a full day's work could never be counted upon. Earlier in the season Grogan's delay would not have been so serious.

But one northeaster as yet had struck the work. This had carried away some of the upper planking, the false work of the coffer-dam ; but this had been repaired in a few hours without delay or serious damage. After that

4

the Indian summer had set in — soft, dreamy days when the winds dozed by the hour, the waves nibbled along the shores, and the swelling breast of the ocean rose and fell as if in gentle slumber.

But would this good weather last? Babcock rose hurriedly, as this anxiety again took possession of him, and leaned over the deck-rail, scanning the sky. He did not like the drift of the low clouds off to the west; southeasters began that way. It looked as though the wind might change.

Some men would not have worried over these possibilities. Babcock did. He was that kind of man.

When the boat touched the shore, he sprang over the chains, and hurried through the ferry-slip.

"Keep an eye out, sir," the bridge-tender called after him, — he had been directing him to Grogan's house, — "perhaps Tom may be on the road."

Then it suddenly occurred to Babcock that, so far as he could remember, he had never seen Mr. Thomas Grogan, his stevedore. He knew Grogan's name, of course, and would have recognized his signature affixed to the little cramped notes with which his orders were always ac-

5

knowledged, but the man himself might have passed unnoticed within three feet of him. This is not unusual where the work of a contractor lies in scattered places, and he must often depend on strangers in the several localities.

As he hurried over the road he recalled the face of Grogan's foreman, a big blond Swede, and that of Grogan's daughter, a slender, fair-haired girl, who once came to the office for her father's pay; but all efforts at reviving the lineaments of Grogan failed.

With this fact clear in his mind, he felt a tinge of disappointment. It would have relieved his temper to unload a portion of it upon the offending stevedore. Nothing cools a man's wrath so quickly as not knowing the size of the head he intends to hit.

As he approached near enough to the sea wall to distinguish the swinging booms and the puffs of white steam from the hoisting-engines, he saw that the main derrick was at work lowering the buckets of mixed concrete to the divers. Instantly his spirits rose. The delay on his contract might not be so serious. Perhaps, after all, Grogan had started work.

When he reached the temporary wooden fence built by the government, shutting off the view of the depot yard, with its coal-docks and machine shops, and neared the small door cut through its planking, a voice rang out clear and strong above the din of the mixers, —

"Hold on, ye wall-eyed macaroni! Do ye want that fall cut? Turn that snatch-block, Cully, and tighten up the watch-tackle. Here, cap'n, lend a hand. Lively now, lively, before I straighten out the hull gang of ye!"

The voice had a ring of unquestioned authority. It was not quarrelsome or abusive or bullying, only earnest and forceful.

"Ease away on that guy! Ease away, I tell ye!" it continued, rising in intensity. "So — all gone! Now, haul out, Cully, and let that other team back up."

Babcock pushed open the door in the fence and stepped in. A loaded scow lay close beside the string-piece of the government wharf. Alongside its forward hatch was rigged a derrick with a swinging gaff. The "fall" led through a snatch-block in the planking of the dock, and operated an iron bucket that was hoisted by a big gray horse driven by a boy. A gang of men were filling these buckets, and a number of teams being loaded with their dumped contents. The captain of the scow was on the dock, holding the guy.

At the foot of the derrick, within ten feet of

7

Babcock, stood a woman perhaps thirty-five years of age, with large, clear, gray eyes, made all the more luminous by the deep, rich color of her sunburnt skin. Her teeth were snow white, and her light brown hair was neatly parted over a wide forehead. She wore a long ulster half concealing her well-rounded, muscular figure, and a black silk hood rolled back from her face, the strings falling over her broad shoulders, revealing a red silk scarf loosely wound about her throat, the two ends tucked in her bosom. Her feet were shod in thick-soled shoes laced around her well-turned ankles, and her hands were covered by buckskin gauntlets creased with wear. From the outside breast pocket of her ulster protruded a time-book, from which dangled a pencil fastened to a hempen string. Every movement indicated great physical strength, perfect health, and a thorough control of herself and her surroundings. Coupled with this was a dignity and repose unmistakable to those who have watched the handling of large bodies of workingmen by some one leading spirit, master in every tone of the voice and every gesture of the body. The woman gave Babcock a quick glance of interrogation as he entered, and, receiving no answer, forgot him instantly.

"Come, now, ye blatherin' dagos," — this

time to two Italian shovellers filling the buckets, — "shall I throw one of ye overboard to
wake ye up, or will I take a hand meself?
Another shovel there — that bucket's not half
full " — drawing one hand from her side pocket
and pointing with an authoritative gesture,
breaking as suddenly into a good-humored laugh
over the awkwardness of their movements.

Babcock — with all his curiosity aroused —
watched her for a moment, forgetting for the
time his own anxieties. He liked a skilled
hand, and he liked push and grit. This woman
seemed to possess all three. He was amazed
at the way in which she handled her men.
He wished somebody as clear-headed and as
capable were unloading his boat. He began to
wonder who she might be. There was no mis-
taking her nationality. Slight as was her ac-
cent, her direct descent from the land of the
shamrock and the shillalah was not to be
doubted. The very tones of her voice seemed
saturated with its national spirit, "A flower for
you when you agree with me, and a broken
head when you don't." But underneath all
these outward indications of dominant power
and great physical strength he detected in the
lines of the mouth and eyes a certain refinement
of nature. There was, too, a fresh, rosy whole-

9

someness, a sweet cleanliness, about the woman.
These, added to the noble lines of her figure,
would have appealed to one as beauty, and only
that, had it not been that the firm mouth, well-
set chin, and deep, penetrating glance of the
eye overpowered all other impressions.

Babcock moved down beside her.

" Can you tell me, madam, where I can find
Thomas Grogan ?"

"Right in front of ye," she answered, turning quickly, with a toss of her head like that
of a great hound baffled in hunt. " I'm Tom
Grogan. What can I do for ye ?"

"Not Grogan the stevedore ?" Babcock
asked in astonishment.

" Yes, Grogan the stevedore. Come! Make
it short, — what can I do for ye ? "

" Then this must be my boat. I came
down " —

" Ye 're not the boss ? " — looking him over
slowly from his feet up, a good-natured smile
irradiating her face, her eyes beaming, every
tooth glistening. " There 's me hand. I 'm
glad to see ye. I 've worked for ye off and on
for four years, and niver laid eyes on ye till this
minute. Don't say a word. I know it. I 've
kept the concrete gangs back half a day, but I
could n't help it. I 've had four horses down

10

with the 'zooty, and two men laid up with dip-
'thery. The Big Gray Cully's drivin' over
there — the one that's a-hoistin' — ain't fit to
be out of the stables. If ye were n't behind in
the work, he'd have two blankets on him this
minute. But I'm here meself now, and I'll
have her out to-night if I work till daylight.
Here, cap'n, pull yerself together. This is the
boss."

Then catching sight of the boy turning a
handspring behind the horse, she called out
again, —

"Now, look here, Cully, none of your sky-
larkin'. There's the dinner whistle. Unhitch
the Big Gray ; he's as dry as a bone."

The boy loosened the traces and led the horse
to water, and Babcock, after a word with the
captain, and an encouraging smile to Tom, turned
away. He meant to go to the engineer's office
before his return to town, now that his affairs
with Grogan were settled. As he swung back
the door in the board fence, he stumbled over
a mere scrap of humanity carrying a dinner
pail. The mite was peering through the crack
and calling to Cully at the horse-trough. He
proved to be a boy of perhaps seven or eight
years of age, but with the face of an old man,
— pinched, weary, and scarred all over with

suffering and pain. He wore a white tennis-cap pulled over his eyes, and a short gray jacket that reached to his waist. Under one arm was a wooden crutch. His left leg was bent at the knee, and swung clear when he jerked his little body along the ground. The other, though unhurt, was thin and bony, the yarn stocking wrinkling over the shrunken calf.

Beside him stood a big billy-goat, harnessed to a two-wheeled cart made of a soap-box.

As Babcock stepped aside to let the boy pass, he heard Cully shouting in answer to the little cripple's cries, "Cheese it, Patsy! Here's Pete Lathers comin' down de yard! Look out fer Stumpy! He'll have his dog on him!"

Patsy laid down the pail and crept through the door again, drawing the crutch after him. The yardmaster passed with a bulldog at his heels, and touching his hat to the contractor, turned the corner of the coal-shed.

"What is your name?" inquired Babcock gently. A cripple always appealed to him, especially a child.

"My name's Patsy, sir," looking straight up into Babcock's eyes, the goat nibbling at his thin hand.

"And who are you looking for?"

"I come down with mother's dinner, sir.

She's here working on the dock. There she is now."

"I thought ye were niver comin' wid that dinner, darlint," came a woman's voice. "What kept ye? Stumpy was tired, was he? Well, niver mind."

The woman lifted the little fellow in her arms, pushed back his cap and smoothed his hair with her fingers, her whole face beaming with tenderness.

"Gimme the crutch, darlint, and hold on to me tight, and we'll get under the shed out of the sun till I see what Jennie's sent me." At this instant she caught Babcock's eye.

"Oh, it's the boss. Sure, I thought ye'd gone back. Pull the hat off ye, me boy; it's the boss we're workin' for, the man that's buildin' the wall. Ye see, sir, when I'm driv' like I am to-day, I can't go home to dinner, and me Jennie sends me — big — man — Patsy — down" — rounding out each word in a pompous tone, as she slipped her hand under the boy's chin and kissed him on the cheek.

After she had propped him between two big spars, she lifted the cover of the tin pail.

"Pigs' feet, as I'm alive, and hot cabbage, and the coffee a-b'ilin' too!" she said, turning to the boy and pulling out a tin flask with a screw top, the whole embedded in the smoking cabbage. "There, we'll be after puttin' it where Stumpy can't be rubbin' his nose in it," —setting the pail, as she spoke, on a rough anchor-stone.

Here the goat moved up, rubbing his head in the boy's face, and then reaching around for the pail.

"Look at him, Patsy! Git out, ye imp, or I'll hurt ye! Leave that kiver alone!" She laughed as she struck at the goat with her empty gauntlet, and shrank back out of the way of his horns.

There was no embarrassment over her informal dinner, eaten as she sat squat in a fence-corner, an anchor-stone for a table, and a pile of spars for a chair. She talked to Babcock in an unabashed, self-possessed way, pouring out the smoking coffee in the flask cup, chewing away on the pigs' feet, and throwing the bones to the goat, who sniffed them contemptuously. "Yes, he's the youngest of our children, sir. He and Jennie — that's home, and 'most as tall as meself — are all that's left. The other two went to heaven when they was little ones."

"Can't the little fellow's leg be straightened?" asked Babcock in a tone which plainly showed his sympathy for the boy's suffering.

"No, not now; so Dr. Mason says. There was a time when it might have been, but I could n't take him. I had him over to Quarantine again two years ago, but it was too late; it 'd growed fast, they said. When he was four years old he would be under the horses' heels all the time, and a-climbin' over them in the stable, and one day the Big Gray fetched him a crack and broke his hip. He did n't mean it, for he 's as dacint a horse as I 've got; but the boys had been a-worritin' him, and he let drive, thinkin', most likely, it was them. He 's been a-hoistin' all the mornin'." Then, catching sight of Cully leading the horse back to work, she rose to her feet, all the fire and energy renewed in her face.

"Shake the men up, Cully! I can't give 'em but half an hour to-day. We 're behind time now. And tell the cap'n to pull them macaronis out of the hold, and start two of 'em to trimmin' some of that stone to starboard. She was a-listin' when we knocked off for dinner. Come, lively!"

II

A BOARD FENCE LOSES A PLANK

THE work on the sea wall progressed. The coffer-dam, which had been built by driving into the mud of the bottom a double row of heavy tongued and grooved planking in two parallel rows, and bulkheading each end with heavy boards, had been filled with concrete to low-water mark, consuming not only the contents of the delayed scow, but two subsequent cargoes, both of which had been unloaded by Tom Grogan.

To keep out the leakage, steam pumps were kept going night and day.

By dint of hard work the upper masonry of the wall had been laid to the top course, ready for the coping, and there was now every prospect that the last stone would be lowered into place before the winter storms set in.

The shanty — a temporary structure, good only for the life of the work — rested on a set of stringers laid on extra piles driven outside of the working platform. When the submarine work lies miles from shore, a shanty is the only shelter for the men, its interior being arranged with sleeping-bunks, with one end partitioned off for a kitchen and a storage-room. This last is filled with perishable property, extra blocks, Manila rope, portable forges, tools, shovels, and barrows.

For this present sea wall — an amphibious sort of structure, with one foot on land and the other in the water — the shanty was of light pine boards, roofed over, and made water-tight by tarred paper. The bunks had been omitted, for most of the men boarded in the village. In this way increased space for the storage of tools was gained, besides room for a desk containing the government working drawings and specifi-cations, pay-rolls, etc. In addition to its door, fastened at night with a padlock, and its one glass window, secured by a tenpenny nail, the shanty had a flap window, hinged at the bot-tom. When this was propped up with a barrel stave it made a counter from which to pay the men, the paymaster standing inside.

Babcock was sitting on a keg of dock spikes inside this working shanty some days after he had discovered Tom's identity, watching his bookkeeper preparing the pay-roll, when a face was thrust through the square of the window.

17

It was not a prepossessing face, rather pudgy and sleek, with uncertain, drooping mouth, and eyes that always looked over one's head when he talked. It was the property of Mr. Peter Lathers, the yardmaster of the depot.

" When you 're done payin' off maybe you 'll step outside, sir," he said in a confiding tone. " I got a friend of mine who wants to know you. He 's a stevedore, and does the work to the fort. He 's never done nothin' for you, but I told him next time you come down I 'd fetch him over. Say, Dan ! " and he beckoned with his head over his shoulder ; then, turning to Babcock, " I make you acquainted, sir, with Mr. Daniel McGaw."

Two faces now filled the window, Lathers's and that of a red-headed man in a straw hat.

" All right. I 'll attend to you in a moment. Glad to see you, Mr. McGaw," said Babcock, rising from the keg, and looking over his book-keeper's shoulder.

Lathers's friend proved to be a short, big-boned, square-shouldered Irishman, about forty years of age, dressed in a once black broadcloth suit with frayed buttonholes, the lapels and vest covered with grease-spots. Around his collar, which had done service for several days, was twisted a red tie decorated with a glass pin. His

18

face was spattered with blue powder-marks, as
if from some quarry explosion. A lump of a
mustache dyed dark brown concealed his upper
lip, making all the more conspicuous the bushy,
sandy-colored eyebrows that shaded a pair of
treacherous eyes. His mouth was coarse and
filled with teeth half worn off, like those of an
old horse. When he smiled these opened slowly
like a vise. Whatever of humor played about
this opening lost its life instantly when these
jaws clicked together again.

The hands were big and strong, wrinkled
and seamed, their rough backs spotted like a
toad's, the wrists covered with long, spidery
hairs.

When he removed his hat Babcock noticed
particularly his low, flat forehead, and the dry,
red hair growing close to the eyebrows.

"I wuz a-sp'akin' to me fri'nd Mister Lathers about doin' yer wurruk," began McGaw,
resting one foot on a pile of barrow-planks, his
elbow on his knee. "I does all the haulin' to
the foort. Surgint Duffy knows me. I wuz
along here las' week, an' see ye wuz put back
fer stone. If I'd had the job, I'd had her unloaded two days befoore."

"You're dead right, Dan," said Lathers,
with an expression of disgust. "This woman

business ain't no good, nohow. She ought to be over her tubs."

"She does her work, though," Babcock said, beginning to see the drift of things.

"Oh, I don't be sayin' she don't. She's a dacint woman, anough; but thim b'ys as is a-runnin' her carts is raisin' h—ll all the toime."

"And then look at the teams," chimed in Lathers, with a jerk of his thumb toward the dock, — "a lot of staggering horse-car wrecks you could n't sell to a glue factory. That big gray she had a-hoistin' is blind of an eye and sprung so forrard he can't hardly stand."

At this moment the refrain of a song from somewhere near the board fence floated through the air, —

"And he wiped up the floor wid McGeechy."

McGaw turned his head in search of the singer, and not finding him, resumed his position.

"What are your rates per ton?" asked Babcock.

"We 're a-chargin' forty cints," said Mc-Gaw, deferring to Lathers, as if for confirmation.

"Who 's ' we ' ?"

"The Stevedores' Union."

"But Mrs. Grogan is doing it for thirty," said Babcock, looking straight into McGaw's eyes, and speaking slowly and deliberately.

"Yis, I heared she wuz a-cuttin' rates; but she can't live at it. If I does it, it'll be done roight, an' no throuble."

"I'll think it over," said Babcock quietly, turning on his heel. The meanness of the whole affair offended him,—two big, strong men vilifying a woman with no protector but her two hands. McGaw should never lift a shovel for him.

Again the song floated out; this time it seemed nearer,—

> . . . "wid McGeechy—
> McGeechy of the Fourth."

"Dan McGaw's giv'n it to you straight," said Lathers, stopping for a last word, his face thrust through the window again. "He's rigged for this business, and Grogan ain't in it with him. If she wants her work done right, she ought to send down something with a mustache."

Here the song subsided in a prolonged chuckle. McGaw turned, and caught sight of a boy's head, with its mop of black hair thrust through a crownless hat, leaning over a water cask. Lathers turned too, and instantly lowered his

21

voice. The head ducked out of sight. In the flash glance Babcock caught of the face, he recognized the boy Cully, Patsy's friend, and the driver of the Big Gray. It was evident to Babcock that Cully at that moment was bubbling over with fun. Indeed, this waif of the streets, sometimes called James Finnegan, was seldom known to be otherwise.

"Thet's the wurrst rat in the stables," said McGaw, his face reddening with anger. "What kin ye do whin ye're a-buckin' ag'in' a lot uv divils loike him ?" — speaking through the window to Babcock. "Come out uv thet," he called to Cully, "or I'll bu'st yer jaw, ye sneakin' rat ! "

Cully came out, but not in obedience to McGaw or Lathers. Indeed, he paid no more attention to either of those distinguished diplomats than if they had been two cement barrels standing on end. His face, too, had lost its irradiating smile ; not a wrinkle or a pucker ruffled its calm surface. His clay-soiled hat was in his hand — a very dirty hand, by the way, with the torn cuff of his shirt hanging loosely over it. His trousers bagged everywhere — at knees, seat, and waist. On his stockingless feet were a pair of sun-baked, brick-colored shoes. His ankles were as dark as mahogany. His throat and chest were

bare, the skin tanned to leather wherever the
sun could work its way through the holes in his
garments. From out of this combination of dust
and rags shone a pair of piercing black eyes,
snapping with fun.

"I come up fer de mont's pay," he said
coolly to Babcock, the corner of his eye glued
tò Lathers. "De ole woman said ye 'd hev it
ready."

"Mrs. Grogan's ?" asked the bookkeeper,
shuffling over his envelopes.

"Yep. Tom Grogan."

"Can you sign the pay-roll ? "

"You bet " — with an eye still out for Lathers.

"Where did you learn to write—at school ? "
asked Babcock, noting the boy's independence
with undisguised pleasure.

"Naw. Patsy an' me studies nights. Pop
Mullins teaches us, — he 's de ole woman's far-
der what she brung out from Ireland. He 's
a-livin' up ter de shebang; dey 're all a-livin'
dere — Jinnie an' de ole woman an' Patsy — all
'cept me an' Carl. I bunks in wid de Big Gray.
Say, mister, ye 'd oughter git onter Patsy; he 's
de little kid wid de crutch. He 's a corker, he
is ; reads po'try an' everythin'. Where 'll I
sign ? Oh, I see ; in dis 'ere square hole right

23

alongside de ole woman's name,'' — spreading his elbows, pen in hand, and affixing '' James Finnegan '' to the collection of autographs. The next moment he was running along the dock, the money envelope tight in his hand, sticking out his tongue at McGaw, and calling to Lathers as he disappeared through the door in the fence, ''Somp'n wid a *mus*tache, somp'n wid a *mus*tache,'' like a newsboy calling an extra. Then a stone grazed Lathers's ear.

Lathers sprang through the gate, but the boy was halfway through the yard. It was this flea-like alertness that always saved Mr. Finnegan's scalp.

Once out of Lathers's reach, Cully bounded up the road like a careering letter X, with arms and legs in air. If there was any one thing that delighted the boy's soul, it was, to quote from his own picturesque vocabulary, '' to set up a job on de ole woman.'' Here was his chance. Before he reached the stable he had planned the whole scene, even to the exact intonation of Lathers's voice when he referred to the dearth of mustaches in the Grogan household. Within a few minutes of his arrival the details of the whole occurrence, word for word, with such picturesque additions as his own fertile imagination could invent, were common talk about the yard.

24

Lathers meanwhile had been called upon to
direct a gang of laborers who were moving an
enormous iron buoy-float down the cinder-cov-
ered path to the dock. Two of the men walked
beside the buoy, steadying it with their hands.
Lathers was leaning against the board fence
of the shop, whittling a stick while the others
worked.

Suddenly there was an angry cry for Lathers,
and every man stood still. So did the buoy and
the moving truck.

With head up, eyes blazing, her silk hood
pushed back from her face, as if to give her air,
her gray ulster open to her waist, her right
hand bare of a glove, came Tom Grogan, brush-
ing the men out of her way.

"I knew I'd find you, Pete Lathers," she
said, facing him squarely; "why do ye want
to be takin' the bread out of me children's
mouths?"

The stick dropped from Lathers's hand.
"Well, who said I did? What have I got to
do with your" —

"You've got enough to do with 'em, you
and your friend McGaw, to want 'em to starve.
Have I ever hurt ye that ye should try an'
sneak me business away from me? Ye know
very well the fight I've made, standin' out on

25

this dock, many a day an' night, in the cold
an' wet, with nothin' between Tom's children
an' the street but these two hands — an' yet
ye 'd slink in like a dog to get me " —

" Here, now, I ain't a-goin' to have no row,"
said Lathers, twitching his shoulders. " It's
against orders, an' I 'll call the yard-watch, and
throw you out if you make any fuss."

" The yard-watch ! " said Tom, with a look of
supreme contempt. " I can handle any two of
'em, an' ye too, an' ye know it." Her cheeks
were aflame. She crowded Lathers so closely
his slinking figure hugged the fence.

By this time the gang had abandoned the
buoy, and were standing aghast, watching the
fury of the Amazon.

" Now, see here, don't make a muss; the
commandant 'll be down here in a minute."

" Let him come ; he 's the one I want to see.
If he knew he had a man in his pay that would
do as dirty a trick to a woman as ye 've done
to me, his name would be Dinnis. I 'll see him
meself this very day, and " — Here Lathers
interrupted with an angry gesture. " Don't ye
lift yer arm at me," she blazed out, " or I 'll
break it at the wrist ! "

Lathers's hand dropped. All the color was
out of his face, his lip quivering.

26

"Whoever said I said a word against you,
Mrs. Grogan, is a —— liar." It was the last
resort of a cowardly nature.

"Stop lyin' to me, Pete Lathers! If there's
anythin' in this world I hate, it's a liar. Ye
said it, and ye know ye said it. Ye want that
drunken loafer Dan McGaw to get me work.
Ye've been at it all summer, an 'ye think I
have n't watched ye ; but I have. And ye say
I don't pay full wages, and have got a lot of
boys to do men's work, an' oughter be over me
tubs. Now let me tell ye " — Lathers shrank
back, cowering before her — "if ever I hear ye
openin' yer head about me, or me teams, or me
work, I 'll make ye swallow every tooth in yer
head. Send down somethin' with a mustache,
will I ? There's not a man in the yard that's
a match for me, an' ye know it. Let one of
'em try that."

Her uplifted fist, tight-clenched, shot past
Lathers's ear. A quick blow, a plank knocked
clear of its fastenings, and a flood of daylight
broke in behind Lathers's head !

"Now, the next time I come, Pete Lathers,"
she said firmly, "I 'll miss the plank and take
yer face."

Then she turned, and stalked out of the
yard.

III

SERGEANT DUFFY'S LITTLE GAME

THE bad weather so long expected finally arrived. An afternoon of soft, warm autumn skies, aglow with the radiance of the setting sun, and brilliant in violet and gold, had been followed by a cold, gray morning. Of a sudden a cloud the size of a hand had mounted clear of the horizon, and called together its fellows. An unseen herald in the east blew a blast, and winds and sea awoke.

By nine o'clock a gale was blowing. By ten Babcock's men were bracing the outer sheathing of the coffer-dam, strengthening the derrick-guys, tightening the anchor-lines, and clearing the working platforms of sand, cement, and other damageable property. The course masonry, fortunately, was above the water-line, but the coping was still unset and the rubble backing of much of the wall unfinished. Two weeks of constant work were necessary before that part of the structure contained in the first section of the contract would be entirely safe for the coming winter. Babcock doubled his gangs, and utilized every hour of low water to the utmost, even when the men stood waist deep. It was his only hope for completing the first section that season. After that would come the cold, freezing the mortar, and ending everything.

Tom Grogan performed wonders. Not only did she work her teams far into the night, but during all this bad weather she stood throughout the day on the unprotected dock, a man's sou'wester covering her head, a rubber waterproof reaching to her feet. She directed every boatload herself, and rushed the materials to the shovellers, who stood soaking wet in the driving rain.

Lathers avoided her ; so did McGaw. Everybody else watched her in admiration. Even the commandant, a bluff, gray-bearded naval officer, —a hero of Hampton Roads and Memphis, —passed her on his morning inspection with a kindly look in his face and an aside to Babcock, " Hire some more like her. She is worth a dozen men."

Not until the final cargo required for the completion of the wall had been dumped on the platforms did she relax her vigilance. Then she shook the water from her oilskins and started

29

for home. During all these hours of constant strain there was no outbreak of bravado, no spell of ill humor. She made no boasts or promises. With a certain buoyant pluck she stood by the derricks day after day, firing volleys of criticism or encouragement, as best suited the exigencies of the moment. Now she sprang forward to catch a sagging bucket, now tended a guy to relieve a man, or handled the teams herself when the line of carts was blocked or stalled.

Every hour she worked increased Babcock's confidence and admiration. He began to feel a certain pride in her, and to a certain extent to rely upon her. Such capacity, endurance, and loyalty were new in his experience. If she owed him anything for her delay on that first cargo, the debt had been amply paid. Yet he saw that no such sense of obligation had influenced her. To her this extra work had been a duty : he was behindhand with the wall, and anxious ; she would help him out. As to the weather, she revelled in it. The dash of the spray and the driving rain only added to her enjoyment. The clatter of rattling buckets and the rhythmic movement of the shovellers keeping time to her orders made a music as dear to her as that of the steady tramp of men and the sound of arms to a division commander.

Owing to the continued bad weather and the difficulty of shipping small quantities of fuel, the pumping-engines ran out of coal, and a complaint from Babcock's office brought the agent of the coal company to the sea wall. In times like these Babcock rarely left his work. Once let the Old Man of the Sea, as he knew, get his finger in between the cracks of a coffer-dam, and he would smash the whole into wreckage.

"I was on my way to see Tom Grogan," said the agent. "I heard you were here, so I stopped to tell you about the coal. There will be a load down in the morning. I am Mr. Crane, of Crane & Co., coal dealers."

"You know Mrs. Grogan, then?" asked Babcock, after the delay in the delivery of the coal had been explained. He had been waiting for some such opportunity to discover more about his stevedore. He never discussed personalities with his men.

"Well, I should say so, — known her for years. Best woman on top of Staten Island. Does she work for you?"

"Yes, and has for some years; but I must confess I never knew Grogan was a woman until I found her on the dock a few weeks ago, handling a cargo. She works like a machine. How long has she been a widow?"

"Well, come to think of it, I don't know that she is a widow. There's some mystery about the old man, but I never knew what. But that don't count; she's good enough as she is, and a hustler, too."

Crane was something of a hustler himself —one of those busy Americans who opens his daily life with an office key and closes it with a letter for the late mail. He was a restless, wiry, black-eyed little man, never still for a moment, and perpetually in chase of another eluding dollar, —which half the time he caught.

Then, laying his hand on Babcock's arm, "And she's square as a brick, too. Sometimes when a chunker captain, waiting to unload, shoves a few tons aboard a sneak-boat at night, Tom will spot him every time. They try to fool her into indorsing their bills of lading in full, but it don't work for a cent."

"You call her Tom Grogan?" Babcock asked, with a certain tone in his voice. He resented, somehow, Crane's familiarity.

"Certainly. Everybody calls her Tom Grogan. It's her husband's name. Call her anything else, and she don't answer. She seems to glory in it, and after you know her a while you don't want to call her anything else yourself. It comes kind of natural, like your calling a man 'colonel' or 'judge.' "

Babcock could not but admit that Crane might be right. All the names which could apply to a woman who had been sweetheart, wife, and mother seemed out of place when he thought of this undaunted spirit who had defied Lathers, and with one blow of her fist sent the splinters of a fence flying about his head.

" We 've got the year's contract for coal at the fort," continued Crane. " The quartermaster sergeant who inspects it — Sergeant Duffy — has a friend named McGaw who wants to do the unloading into the government bins. There 's a low price on the coal, and there 's no margin for anybody ; and if Duffy should kick about the quality of the coal, — and you can't please these fellows if they want to be ugly, — Crane & Co. will be in a hole, and lose money on the contract. I hate to go back on Tom Grogan, but there 's no help for it. The ten cents a ton I 'd save if she hauls the coal instead of McGaw would be eaten up in Duffy's short weights and rejections. I sent Sergeant Duffy's letter to her, so she can tell how the land lies, and I 'm going up now to her house to see her, on my way to the fort. I don't know what Duffy will get out of it; perhaps he gets a few dollars out of

33

the hauling. The coal is shipped, by the way, and ought to be here any minute."

"Wait; I'll go with you," said Babcock, handing him an order for more coal. "She hasn't sent down the tally sheet for my last scow." There was not the slightest necessity, of course, for Babcock to go to Grogan's house for this document.

As they walked on, Crane talked of everything except what was uppermost in Babcock's mind. Babcock tried to lead the conversation back to Tom, but Crane's thoughts were on something else.

When they reached the top of the hill, the noble harbor lay spread out beneath them, from the purple line of the great cities to the silver sheen of the sea inside the narrows. The clearing wind had hauled to the northwest. The sky was heaped with soft clouds floating in the blue. At the base of the hill nestled the buildings and wharves of the Lighthouse Depot, with the unfinished sea wall running out from the shore, fringed with platforms and bristling with swinging booms — the rings of white steam twirling from the exhaust-pipes.

On either side of the vast basin lay two grim, silent forts, crouched on grassy slopes like great beasts with claws concealed. Near by,

big lazy steamers, sullen and dull, rested motionless at quarantine, awaiting inspection; while
beyond, white-winged graceful yachts curved
tufts of foam from their bows. In the open,
elevators rose high as church steeples; long
lines of canal-boats stretched themselves out
like huge water-snakes, with hissing tugs for
heads; enormous floats groaned under whole
trains of cars; big, burly lighters drifted slowly
with widespread oil-stained sails; monster derricks towered aloft, derricks that pick up a hun-
dred-ton gun as easily as an ant does a grain of
sand, — each floating craft made necessary by
some special industry peculiar to the port of
New York, and each unlike any other craft in
the harbor of any other city of the world.

Grogan's house and stables lay just over the
brow of this hill, in a little hollow. The house
was a plain, square frame dwelling, with front
and rear verandas, protected by the arching
branches of a big sycamore-tree, and surrounded
by a small garden filled with flaming dahlias
and chrysanthemums. Everything about the
place was scrupulously neat and clean.

The stables — there were two — stood on
the lower end of the lot. They looked new, or
were newly painted in a dark red, and appeared
to have accommodations for a number of horses.

35

The stable yard lay below the house. In its open square were a pump and a horse-trough, at which two horses were drinking. One, the Big Gray, had his collar off, showing where the sweat had discolored the skin, the traces crossed loosely over his back. He was drinking eagerly, and had evidently just come in from work. About, under the sheds, were dirt-carts tilted forward on their shafts, and dust-begrimed harnesses hanging on wooden pegs.

A strapping young fellow in a red shirt came out of the stable door, leading two other horses to the trough. Babcock looked about him in surprise at the extent of the establishment. He had supposed that his stevedore had a small outfit, and needed all the work she could get. If, as McGaw had said, only boys did Grogan's work, they at least did it well.

Crane mounted the porch first and knocked. Babcock followed.

"No, Mr. Crane," said a young girl, opening the door, "she's not at home. I'm expecting her every minute. Mother went to work early this morning. She'll be sorry to miss you, sir. She ought to be home now, for she's been up 'most all night at the fort. She's just sent Carl up for two more horses. Won't you come in and wait?"

"No; I'll keep on to the fort," answered Crane. "I may meet her on the road."

"May I come in?" Babcock asked, explaining his business in a few words.

"Oh, yes, sir. Mother won't be long now. You've not forgotten me, Mr. Babcock? I'm her daughter, Jennie. I was to your office once. Gran'pop, this is the gentleman mother works for."

An old man rose with some difficulty from an armchair, and bowed in a kindly, deferential way. He had been reading near the window. He was in his shirt-sleeves, his collar open at the throat. He seemed rather feeble. His legs shook as if he were weak from some recent illness. About the eyes was a certain kindliness that did not escape Babcock's quick glance; they were clear and honest, and looked straight into his — the kind he liked. The old man's most striking features were his silver-white hair, parted over his forehead and falling to his shoulders, and his thin, straight, transparent nose, indicating both ill health and a certain refinement and sensitiveness of nature. Had it not been for his dress, he might have passed for an English curate on half pay.

"Me name's Richard, sor — Richard Mullins," said the old man. "I'm Mary's father.

37

She won't be long gone now. She promised me she 'd be home for dinner.'' He placed a chair for Babcock, and remained standing.

"I will wait until she returns," said Babcock. He had come to discover something more definite about this woman who worked like a steam-engine, crooned over a cripple, and broke a plank with her fist, and he did not intend to leave until he knew. "Your daughter must have had great experience. I have never seen any one man handle work better," he continued, extending his hand. Then, noticing that Mullins was still standing, "Don't let me take your seat."

Mullins hesitated, glanced at Jennie, and without replying moved another chair from the window, drew it nearer, and settled slowly beside Babcock.

The room was as clean as bare arms and scrubbing brushes could make it. Near the fireplace was a cast-iron stove, and opposite this stood a parlor organ, its top littered with photographs. A few chromos hung on the walls. There were also a big plush sofa and two haircloth rocking-chairs, of walnut, covered with cotton tidies. The carpet on the floor was new, and in the window, where the old man had been sitting, some pots of nasturtiums were blooming, their tendrils reaching up both sides of the sash. Opening from this room was the kitchen, resplendent in bright pans and a shining copper wash-boiler. The girl passed constantly in and out the open door, spreading the cloth and bringing dishes for the table.

Her girlish figure was clothed in a blue calico frock and white apron, the sleeves rolled up to the elbows, showing some faint traces of flour clinging to her wrists, as if she had been suddenly summoned from the bread-bowl. She was fresh and sweet, strong and healthy, with a certain grace of manner about her that pleased Babcock instantly. He saw now that she had her mother's eyes and color, but not her air of fearlessness and self-reliance, that kind of self-reliance which comes only of many nights of anxiety and many days of success. He noticed, too, that when she spoke to the old man her voice was tempered with a peculiar tenderness, as if his infirmities were more to be pitied than complained of. This pleased him most of all.

"You live with your daughter, Mrs. Grogan ? " Babcock asked in a friendly way, turning to the old man.

"Yis, sor. Whin Tom got sick, she sint fer me to come over an' hilp her. I feeds the horses

39

whin Oi 'm able, an' looks after the garden,
but Oi 'm not much good."

" Is Mr. Thomas Grogan living ? " asked
Babcock cautiously, and with a certain tone of
respect, hoping to get closer to the facts, and
yet not to seem intrusive.

" Oh, yis, sor; an' moight be dead fer all
the good he does. He 's in New Yorruk some-
'er's, on a farm " — lowering his voice to a
whisper, and looking anxiously toward Jennie
— " belongin' to the State, I think, sor. He 's
hurted pretty bad, an' p'haps he 's a leetle off
— I dunno. Mary has niver tould me."

Before Babcock could pursue the inquiry further there was a firm tread on the porch steps,
and the old man rose from the chair, his face
brightening.

" Here she is, Grand'pop," said Jennie, laying down her dish and springing to the door.

" Hold tight, darlint," came a voice from the
outside, and the next instant Tom Grogan strode
in, her face aglow with laughter, her hood awry,
her eyes beaming. Patsy was perched on her
shoulder, his little crutch fast in one hand, the
other tightly wound about her neck. " Let go,
darlint ; ye 're a-chokin' the wind out of me.

" Oh, it 's ye a-waitin', Mr. Babcock; me
man Carl thought ye 'd gone. Mr. Crane I met

"OH, IT'S YE A-WAITIN', MR. BABCOCK."

outside told me you'd been here. Jennie'll
get the tally-sheet of the last load for ye. I've
been to the fort since daylight, and pretty much
all night, to tell ye God's truth. Oh, Gran'-
pop, but I smashed 'em!" she exclaimed as
she gently removed Patsy's arm and laid him
in the old man's lap. She had picked the little
cripple up at the garden gate, where he always
waited for her. "That's the last job that
sneakin' Duffy and Dan McGaw'll ever put up
on me. Oh, but ye should 'a' minded the face
on him, Gran'pop!" — untying her hood and
breaking into a laugh so contagious in its mirth
that even Babcock joined in without knowing
what it was all about.

As she spoke, Tom stood facing her father,
hood and ulster off, the light of the windows
silhouetting the splendid lines of her well-
rounded figure, with its deep chest, firm bust,
broad back, and full throat, her arms swinging
loose and free.

"Ye see," she said, turning to Babcock,
"that man Duffy tried to do me — he's the
sergeant at the fort — and Dan McGaw, — ye
know him; he's the divil that wanted to work
for ye. Ye know I always had the hauling of
the coal at the fort, an' I want to hold on to it,
for it comes every year. I've been a-watchin'

41

for this coal for a month. Every October there's a new contractor, and this time it was me friend Mr. Crane I 've worked for before. So I sees Duffy about it the other day, an' he says, 'Well, I think ye better talk to the quartermaster, who 's away, but who 'll be home next week.' An' that night when I got home, there lay a letter from Mr. Crane, wid another letter inside it Sergeant Duffy had sent to Mr. Crane, sayin' he 'd recommend Dan McGaw to do the stevedorin' — the sneakin' villain — an' sayin' that he, Duffy, was a-goin' to inspect the coal himself, an' if his friend Dan McGaw hauled it, the quality would be all right. Think of that! I tell ye, Mr. Babcock, they 're divils. Then Mr. Crane put down at the bottom of his letter to me that he was sorry not to give me the job, but that he must give it to Duffy's friend McGaw, or Duffy might reject the coal. Wait till I wash me hands and I 'll tell ye how I fixed him," she added suddenly, as with a glance at her fingers she disappeared into the kitchen, reappearing a moment later with her bare arms as fresh and as rosy as her cheeks, from their friction with a clean crash towel.

"Well!" she continued, "I jumps into me bonnet yesterday, and over I goes to the fort; an' I up an' says to Duffy, 'I can't wait for the

quartermaster. When 's that coal a-comin' ? '
An' he says, ' In a couple of weeks.' An' I
turned onto him and says, ' Ye 're a pretty
loafer to take the bread out of Tom Grogan's
children's mouths! An' ye want Dan McGaw
to do the haulin', do ye ? An' the quality of
the coal 'll be all right if he gits it ? An' there 's
sure to be twenty-five dollars for ye, won't
there ? If I hear a word more out of ye I 'll see
Colonel Howard sure, an' hand him this letter.'
An' Duffy turned white as a load of lime, and
says, ' Don't do it, for God's sake ! It 'll cost me
m' place.' While I was a-talkin' I see a chunk-
er-boat with the very coal on it round into the
dock with a tug ; an' I ran to the string-piece
and catched the line, and has her fast to a spile
before the tug lost headway. Then I started
for home on the run, to get me derricks and
stuff. I got home, hooked up by twelve o'clock
last night, an' before daylight I had me rig up
an' the fall set and the buckets over her hatches.
At six o'clock this mornin' I took the teams
and was a-runnin' the coal out of the chunker,
when down comes Mr. — Daniel — McGaw
with a gang and his big derrick on a cart.'' She
repeated this in a mocking tone, swinging her
big shoulders exactly as her rival would have
done.

'"'That's me rig,' I says to him, p'intin' up
to the gaff, 'an' me coal, an' I'll throw the
fust man overboard who lays hands on it!'
An' then the sergeant come out and took Mc-
Gaw one side an' said somethin' to him, with
his back to me; an' when McGaw turned he
was white too, an' without sayin' a word he
turned the team and druv off. An' just now I
met Mr. Crane walkin' down, lookin' like he
had lost a horse. 'Tom Grogan,' he says, 'I
hate to disappoint ye, an' would n't, for ye've
always done me work well; but I'm stuck on
the coal contract, an' the sergeant can put me
in a hole if ye do the haulin'.' An' I says,
'Brace up, Mr. Crane, there's a hole, but ye
ain't in it, an' the sergeant is. I'll unload every
pound of that coal, if I do it for nothin', and if
that sneak in striped trousers bothers me or you,
I'll pull him apart an' stamp on him!'"

Through all her talk there was a triumphant
good humor, a joyousness, a glow and breezi-
ness, which completely fascinated Babcock.
Although she had been up half the night, she
was as sweet and fresh and rosy as a child.
Her vitality, her strength, her indomitable energy, impressed him as no woman's had ever
done before.

When she had finished her story she suddenly caught Patsy out of her father's arms and dropped with him into a chair, all the mother-hunger in her still unsatisfied. She smoth-ered him with kisses and hugged him to her breast, holding his pinched face against her ruddy cheek. Then she smoothed his forehead with her well-shaped hand, and rocked him back and forth. By and by she told him of the stone that the Big Gray had got in his hoof down at the fort that morning, and how lame he had been, and how Cully had taken it out with — a — great — big — spike ! — dwelling on the last words as if they belonged to some wonderful fairy-tale. The little fellow sat up in her lap and laughed as he patted her breast joyously with his thin hand. " Cully could do it," he shouted in high glee ; " Cully can do anything." Babcock, apparently, made no more difference to her than if he had been an extra chair.

As she moved about her rooms afterward, calling to her men from the open door, consult-ing with Jennie, her arms about her neck, or stopping at intervals to croon over her child, she seemed to him to lose all identity with the wo-man on the dock. The spirit that enveloped her belonged rather to that of some royal dame of heroic times, than to that of a working-woman

45

of to-day. The room somehow became her cas-
tle, the rough stablemen her knights.

On his return to his work she walked back
with him part of the way. Babcock, still bewildered, and still consumed with curiosity to
learn something of her past, led the talk to her
life along the docks, expressing his great surprise at discovering her so capable and willing
to do a man's work, asking who had taught her,
and whether her husband in his time had been
equally efficient and strong.

Instantly she grew reticent. She did not even
answer his question. He waited a moment, and,
realizing his mistake, turned the conversation in
another direction.

" And how about those rough fellows around
the wharves, — those who don't know you, —
are they never coarse and brutal to you?"

" Not when I look 'em in the face," she answered slowly and deliberately. " No man ever
opens his head, nor dar's n't. When they see
me a-comin' they stops talkin', if it's what
they would n't want their daughters to hear;
an' there ain't no dirty back talk, neither. An'
I make me own men civil, too, with a dacint
tongue in their heads. I had a young strip of a
lad once who would be a-swearin' round the
stables. I told him to mend his manners or I'd

wash his mouth out, an' that I would n't have nobody hit me horses on the head. He kep' along, an' I see it was a bad example for the other drivers (this was only a year ago, an' I had three of 'em) ; so when he hit the Big Gray ag'in, I hauled off and give him a crack that laid him out. I was scared solid for two hours, though they never knew it."

Then, with an almost piteous look in her face, and with a sudden burst of confidence, born, doubtless, of a dawning faith in the man's evident sincerity and esteem, she said in a faltering tone, —

"God help me ! what can I do ? I 've no man to stand by me, an' somebody 's got to be boss."

IV

A WALKING DELEGATE LEARNS A NEW STEP

McGAW'S failure to undermine Tom's business with Babcock, and his complete discomfiture over Crane's coal contract at the fort, only intensified his hatred of the woman.

Finding that he could make no headway against her alone, he called upon the Union to assist him, claiming that she was employing non-union labor, and had thus been able to cut down the discharging rates to starvation prices.

A meeting was accordingly called by the executive committee of the Knights, and a resolution passed condemning certain persons in the village of Rockville as traitors to the cause of the workingman. Only one copy of this edict was issued and mailed. This found its way into Tom Grogan's letter-box. Five minutes after she had broken the seal, her men discovered the document pasted upside down on her stable door.

McGaw heard of her action that night, and

48

started another line of attack. It was managed
so skilfully that that which until then had been
only a general dissatisfaction over Tom's business methods on the part of the members of the
Union and their sympathizers now developed
into an avowed determination to crush her.
They discussed several plans by which she could
be compelled either to restore rates for unloading, or be forced out of the business altogether.
As one result of these deliberations a committee
called upon the priest, Father McCluskey, and
informed him of the delicate position in which
the Union had been placed by her having hidden
her husband away, thus forcing them to fight
the woman herself. She was making trouble,
they urged, with her low wages and her unloading rates. "Perhaps his Riverence c'u'd
straighten her out."

Father McCluskey's interview with Tom took
place in the priest's room one morning after
early mass. It had gone abroad, somehow, that
his Reverence intended to discipline the "high-
flyer," and a considerable number of the "tenement-house gang," as Tom called them, had
loitered behind to watch the effect of the good
father's remonstrances.

What Tom told the priest no one ever knew :
such conferences are part of the régime of the

church, and go no farther. It was noticed, however as she came down the aisle, that her eyes were red, as if from weeping, and that she never raised them from the floor as she passed between her enemies on her way to the church door. Once outside she put her arm around Jennie, who was waiting, and the two strolled slowly across the lots to her house.

When the priest came out, his own eyes were tinged with moisture. He called Dennis Quigg, McGaw's right-hand man, and in a voice loud enough to be heard by those nearest him expressed his indignation that any dissension should have arisen among his people over a woman's work, and said that he would hear no more of this unchristian and unmanly interference with one whose only support came from the labor of her hands.

McGaw and his friends were not discouraged. They were only determined upon some more definite stroke. It was therefore ordered that a committee be appointed to waylay her men going to work, and inform them of their duty to their fellow laborers.

Accordingly, this same Quigg — smooth-shaven, smirking, and hollow-eyed, with a diamond pin, half a yard of watch chain, and a fancy shirt, ex-village clerk with his accounts short, ex-deputy sheriff with his accounts of cruelty and blackmail long, and at present walking delegate of the Union — was appointed a committee of one for that duty.

Quigg began by begging a ride in one of Tom's return carts, and taking this opportunity to lay before the driver the enormity of working for Grogan, for thirty dollars a month and board, when there were a number of his brethren out of work and starving who would not work for less than two dollars a day if it were offered them. It was plainly the driver's duty, Quigg urged, to give up his job until Tom Grogan could be compelled to hire him back at advanced wages. During this enforced idleness the Union would pay the driver fifty cents a day. Here Quigg pounded his chest, clenched his fists, and said solemnly, " If capital once downs the lab'rin' man, we 'll all be slaves."

The driver was Carl Nilsson, a Swede, a big, blue-eyed, light-haired young fellow of twenty-two, a sailor from boyhood, who three years before, on a public highway, had been picked up penniless and hungry by Tom Grogan, after the keeper of a sailors' boarding-house had robbed him of his year's savings. The change from cracking ice from a ship's deck with a marline spike, to currying and feeding something

51

alive and warm and comfortable, was so delightful to the Swede that he had given up the sea
for a while. He had felt that he could ship again
at any time, the water was so near. As the
months went by, however, he too, gradually
fell under the spell of Tom's influence. She reminded him of the great Norse women he had
read about in his boyhood. Besides all this, he
was loyal and true to the woman who had be-
friended him, and who had so far appreciated
his devotion to her interests as to promote him
from hostler and driver to foreman of the stables.

Nilsson knew Quigg by sight, for he had
seen him walking home with Jennie from church.
His knowledge of English was slight, but it was
enough to enable him to comprehend Quigg's
purpose as he talked beside him on the cart.
After some questions about how long the enforced idleness would continue, he asked suddenly, —

" Who da horse clean when I go 'way ? "

" D—n her ! let her clean it herself," Quigg
answered angrily.

This ended the question for Nilsson, and it
very nearly ended the delegate. Jumping from
the cart, Carl picked up the shovel and sprang
toward Quigg, who dodged out of his way, and
then took to his heels.

When Nilsson, still white with anger, reached the dock, he related the incident to Cully, who on his return home retailed it to Jennie with such variety of gesture and intonation that that young lady blushed scarlet, but whether from sympathy for Quigg or admiration for Nilsson, Cully was unable to decide.

Quigg's failure to coax away one of Tom's men ended active operations against Tom, so far as the Union was concerned. It continued to listen to McGaw's protests, but, with an eye open for its own interests, replied that if Grogan's men would not be enticed away it could at present take no further action. His trouble with Tom was an individual matter, and a little patience on McGaw's part was advised. The season's work was over, and nothing of importance could be done until the opening of the spring business. If Tom's men struck now, she would be glad to get rid of them. It would, therefore, be wiser to wait until she could not do without them, when they might all be forced out in a body. In the interim McGaw should direct his efforts to harassing his enemy. Perhaps a word with Slattery, the blacksmith, might induce that worthy brother Knight to refuse to do her shoeing some morning when she was stalled for want of a horse; or he might

53

let a nail slip in a tender hoof. No one could tell what might happen in the coming months. At the moment the funds of the Union were too low for aggressive measures. Were McGaw, however, to make a contribution of two hundred dollars to the bank account in order to meet possible emergencies, something might be done. All this was duly inscribed in the books of the committee, — that is, the last part of it; and upon McGaw's promising to do what he could toward improving the funds, it was thereupon subsequently resolved that before resorting to harsher measures the Union should do all in its power toward winning over the enemy. Brother Knight Dennis Quigg was thereupon deputed to call upon Mrs. Grogan and invite her into the Union.

On brother Knight Dennis Quigg's declining for private reasons the honorable mission intrusted to him by the honorable board (Mr. Quigg's exact words of refusal, whispered in the chairman's ear, were, " I 'm a-jollyin' one of her kittens; send somebody else after the old cat "), another walking delegate, brother Knight Crimmins by name, was selected to carry out the gracious action of the committee.

Crimmins had begun life as a plumber's helper, had been iceman, night watchman,

54

heeler, and full-fledged plumber ; and having been out of work himself for months at a time, was admirably qualified to speak of the advantages of idleness to any other candidate for like honors.

He was a small man with a big nose, grizzled chin whiskers, and rum and watery eyes, and wore constantly a pair of patched blue overalls as a badge of his laborship. The seat of these outside trousers showed more wear than his hands.

Immediately upon his appointment, Crimmins went to McGaw's house to talk over the line of attack. The conference was held in the sitting-room and behind closed doors — so tightly closed that young Billy McGaw, with one eye in mourning from the effect of a recent street fight, was unable, even by the aid of the undamaged eye and the keyhole, to get the slightest inkling of what was going on inside.

When the door was finally opened and Mc-Gaw and Crimmins came out, they brought with them an aroma the pungency of which was explained by two empty glasses and a black bottle decorating one end of the only table in the room.

As Crimmins stepped down from the broken stoop, with its rusty rain-spout and rotting floor planks, Billy overheard this parting remark from his father : " Thry the ile furst, Crimmy, an' see what she 'll do ; thin give her the vinegar ; and thin," with an oath, " ef that don't fetch 'er, come back here to me and we 'll give 'er the red pepper."

Brother Knight Crimmins waved his hand to the speaker. " Just leave 'er to me, Dan," he said, and started for Tom's house. Crimmins was delighted with his mission. He felt sure of bringing back her application within an hour. Nothing ever pleased him so much as to work a poor woman into an agony of fright with threats of the Union. Wives and daughters had often followed him out into the street, begging him to let the men alone for another week, until they could pay the rent. Sometimes, when he relented, the more grateful would bless him for his magnanimity. This increased his self-respect.

Tom met him at the door. She had been sitting up with a sick child of Dick Todd, foreman at the brewery, and had just come home. Hardly a week passed without some one in distress sending for her. She had never seen Crimmins before, and thought he had come to mend the roof. His first words, however, betrayed him.

"The Knights sent me up to have a word wid ye."

Tom made a movement as if to shut the door in his face; then she paused for an instant, and said curtly, "Come inside."

Crimmins crushed his slouch hat in his hand, and slunk into a chair by the window. Tom remained standing.

"I see ye like flowers, Mrs. Grogan," he began in his gentlest voice. "Them geraniums is the finest I iver see," peering under the leaves of the plants. "Guess it's 'cause ye water 'em so much."

Tom made no reply.

Crimmins fidgeted on his chair a little, and tried another tack. "I s'pose ye ain't doin' much just now, weather's so bad. The road's awful goin' down to the fort."

Tom's hands were in the side pockets of her ulster. Her face was aglow with her brisk walk from the tenements. She never took her eyes from his face, and never moved a muscle of her body. She was slowly revolving in her mind whether any information she could get out of him would be worth the waiting for.

Crimmins relapsed into silence, and began patting the floor with his foot. The prolonged stillness was becoming uncomfortable.

"I was tellin' ye about the meetin' we had
to the Union last night. We was goin' over the
list of members, an' we did n't find yer name.
The board thought maybe ye 'd like to come
in wid us. The dues is only two dollars a
month. We 're a-regulatin' the prices for next
year, stevedorin' an' haulin', an' the rates 'll
be sent out next week." The stopper was now
out of the oil bottle.

"How many members have ye got?" she
asked quietly.

"Hundred an' seventy-three in our branch
of the Knights."

"All pay two dollars a month?"

"That 's about the size of it," said Crimmins.

"What do we git when we jine?"

"Well, we all pull together — that 's one
thing. One man's strike 's every man's strike.
The capitalists been tryin' to down us, an' the
laborin'-man 's got to stand together. Did ye
hear about the Fertilizer Company 's layin' off
two of our men las' Friday just fer bein' off
a day or so without leave, and their gittin' a
couple of scabs from Hoboken to" —

"What else do we git?" demanded Tom,
in a quick, imperious tone, ignoring the digres-
sion. She had moved a step closer.

Crimmins looked slyly up into her eyes. Until this moment he had been addressing his remarks to the brass ornament on the extreme top of the cast-iron stove. Tom's expression of face did not reassure him ; in fact, the steady gaze of her clear gray eye was as uncomfortable as the focused light of a sun lens.

" Well — we help each other," he blurted out.

" Do *you* do any helpin' ? "

" Yis," stiffening a little. " I 'm the walkin' delegate of our branch."

" Oh, ye 're the walkin' delegate ! *You* don't pay no two dollars, then, do ye ? "

" No. There 's got to be somebody a-goin' round all the time, an' Dinnis Quigg and me 's confidential agents of the branch, an' *what we says goes*," slapping his overalls decisively with his fist. McGaw's suggested stopper was being loosened on the vinegar.

Tom's fingers closed tightly. Her collar began to feel small. " An' I s'pose if ye said I should pay me men double wages, and put up the price o' haulin' so high that me customers could n't pay it, so that some of yer dirty loafers could cut in an' git it, I 'd have to do it, whether I wanted to or not ; or maybe ye think I 'd oughter chuck some o' me own boys into the

59

road because they don't belong to yer branch,
as ye call it, and git a lot o' dead beats to work
in their places who don't know a horse from
a coal-bucket. An' ye'll help me, will ye?
Come out here on the front porch, Mr. Crimmins," opening the door with a jerk. "Do ye
see that stable over there? Well, it covers
seven horses; an' the shed has six carts with
all the harness. Back of it — perhaps if ye
stand on yer toes even a little feller like you
can see the top of another shed. That one has
me derricks an' tools."

Crimmins tried to interrupt long enough to
free McGaw's red pepper, but her words poured
out in a torrent.

"Now ye can go back an' tell Dan McGaw
an' the balance of yer two-dollar loafers that
there ain't a dollar owin' on any horse in my
stable, an' that I've earned everything I've
got without a man round to help 'cept those I
pays wages to. An' ye can tell 'em, too, that
I'll hire who I please, an' pay 'em what they
oughter git; an' I'll do me own haulin' an'
unloadin' fer nothin' if it suits me. When ye
said ye were a walkin' delegate ye spoke God's
truth. Ye'd be a ridin' delegate if ye could;
but there's one thing ye'll niver be, an' that's
a workin' delegate, as long as ye kin find fools

to pay ye wages fer bummin' round day 'n' night. If I had me way, ye *would* walk, but it would be on yer uppers, wid yer bare feet to the road."

Crimmins again attempted to speak, but she raised her arm threateningly. "Now, if it's walkin' ye are, ye can begin right away. Let me see ye earn yer wages down that garden an' into the road. Come, lively now, before I disgrace meself a-layin' hands on the likes of ye!"

V

A WORD FROM THE TENEMENTS

ONE morning Patsy came up the garden path limping on his crutch; the little fellow's eyes were full of tears. He had been out with his goat when some children from the tenements surrounded his cart, pitched it into the ditch, and followed him halfway home, calling "Scab! scab!" at the top of their voices.

Cully heard his cries, and ran through the yard to meet him, his anger rising at every step. To lay hands on Patsy was, to Cully, the unpardonable sin. Ever since the day, five years before, when Tom had taken him into her employ, a homeless waif of the streets, — his father had been drowned from a canal-boat she was unloading, — and had set him down beside Patsy's crib to watch while she was at her work, Jennie being at school, Cully had loved the little cripple with the devotion of a dog to its master. Lawless, rough, often cruel, and sometimes vindictive as Cully was to others, a word from Patsy humbled and softened him.

And Patsy loved Cully. His big, broad chest, stout, straight legs, strong arms and hands, were his admiration and constant pride. Cully was his champion and his ideal. The waif's recklessness and audacity were to him only evidences of so much brains and energy.

This love between the lads grew stronger after Tom had sent to Dublin for her old father, that she might have "a man about the house." Then a new blessing came, not only into the lives of both the lads, but into the whole household as well. Mullins, in his later years, had been a dependent about Trinity College, and constant association with books and students had given him a taste for knowledge denied his daughter. Tom had left home when a girl. In the long winter nights during the slack season, after the stalls were bedded and the horses were fed and watered and locked up for the night, the old man would draw up his chair to the big kerosene lamp on the table, and tell the boys stories — they listening with wide-open eyes, Cully interrupting the narrative every now and then by such asides as "No flies on them fellers, wuz ther', Patsy? They wuz daisies, they wuz. Go on, Pop; it's better'n a circus;" while Patsy would cheer aloud at the downfall of the vanquished, with

63

their "three thousand lance-bearers put to death by the sword," waving his crutch over his head in his enthusiasm.

Jennie would come in too, and sit by her mother; and after Nilsson's encounter with Quigg —an incident which greatly advanced him in Tom's estimation — Cully would be sent to bring him in from his room over the stable and give him a chair with the others, that he might learn the language easier. At these times it was delightful to watch the expression of pride and happiness that would come over Tom's face as she listened to her father's talk.

"But ye have a great head, Gran'pop," she would say. "Cully, ye blatherin' idiot, why don't ye brace up an' git some knowledge in yer head? Sure, Gran'pop, Father McCluskey ain't in it wid ye a minute. Ye could down the whole gang of 'em." And the old man would smile faintly and say he had heard the young gentlemen at the college recite the stories so many times he could never forget them.

In this way the boys grew closer together, Patsy cramming himself from books during the day in order to tell Cully at night all about the Forty Thieves boiled in oil, or Ali Baba and his donkey, or poor man Friday to whom Robinson Crusoe was so kind; and Cully relating in return how Jimmie Finn smashed Pat Gilsey's face because he threw stones at his sister, ending with a full account of a dog-fight which a "snoozer of a cop" stopped with his club.

So when Patsy came limping up the garden path this morning, rubbing his eyes, his voice choking, and the tears streaming, and, burying his little face in Cully's jacket, poured out his tale of insult and suffering, that valiant defender of the right pulled his cap tight over his eyes and began a still hunt through the tenements. There, as he afterwards expressed it, he "mopped up the floor" with one after another of the ringleaders, beginning with young Billy McGaw, Dan's eldest son and Cully's senior.

Tom was dumbfounded at the attack on Patsy. This was a blow upon which she had not counted. To strike her Patsy, her cripple, her baby! The cowardice of it incensed her. She knew instantly that her affairs must have been common talk about the tenements to have produced so great an effect upon the children. She felt sure that their fathers and mothers had encouraged them in it.

In emergencies like this it was never to the old father that she turned. He was too feeble, too much a thing of the past. While to a certain extent he influenced her life, standing

always for the right and always for the kindest
thing she could do, yet when it came to times of
action and danger she felt the need of a younger
and more vigorous mind. It was on Jennie, really
more her companion than her daughter, that she
depended for counsel and sympathy at these
times.

Tom did not underestimate the gravity of the
situation. Up to that point in her career she
had fought only the cold, the heat, the many
weary hours of labor far into the night, and now
and then some man like McGaw. But this stab
from out the dark was a danger to which she
was unused. She saw in this last move of Mc-
Gaw's, aided as he was by the Union, not only
a determination to ruin her, but a plan to divide
her business among a set of men who hated her
as much on account of her success as for anything else. A few more horses and carts and
another barn or two, and she herself would become a hated capitalist. That she had stood out
in the wet and cold herself, hours at a time, like
any man among them; that she had, in her
husband's early days, helped him feed and bed
their one horse, often currying him herself;
that when she and her Tom had moved to Rockville with their savings and there were three
horses to care for and her husband needed more

help than he could hire, she had brought her
little baby Patsy to the stable while she worked
there like a man ; that during all this time she
had cooked and washed and kept the house tidy
for four people ; that she had done all these
things she felt would not count now with the
Union, though each member of it was a bread-
winner like herself.

She knew what power it wielded. There had
been the Martin family, honest, hard-working
people, who had come down from Haverstraw
— the man and wife and their three children —
and moved into the new tenement with all their
nice furniture and new carpets. Tom had helped
them unload these things from the brick-sloop
that brought them. A few weeks after, poor
Martin, still almost a stranger, had been brought
home from the gas-house with his head laid
open, because he had taken the place of a Union
man discharged for drunkenness, and lingered
for weeks until he died. Then the widow, with
her children about her, had been put aboard
another sloop that was going back to her old
home. Tom remembered, as if it were yesterday, the heap of furniture and little pile of
kitchen things sold under the red flag outside
the store near the post-office.

She had seen, too, the suffering and misery

of her neighbors during the long strike at the brewery two years before, and the moving in and out from house to tenement and tenement to shanty, with never a day's work afterward for any man who left his job. She had helped many of the men who, three years before, had been driven out of work by the majority vote of the Carpenters' Union, and who dared not go back and face the terrible excommunication, the social boycott, with all its insults and cruelties. She shuddered as she thought again of her suspicions years ago when the bucket had fallen that crushed in her husband's chest, and sent him to bed for months, only to leave it a wrecked man. The rope that held the bucket had been burned by acid, Dr. Mason said. Some grudge of the Union, she had always felt, was paid off then.

She knew what the present trouble meant, now that it was started, and she knew in what it might end. But her courage never wavered. She ran over in her mind the names of the several men who were fighting her, — McGaw, for whom she had a contempt ; Dempsey and Jimmie Brown, of the executive committee, both liquor dealers ; Paterson, foreman of the gashouse ; and the rest — dangerous enemies, she knew.

A WORD FROM THE TENEMENTS

That night she sent for Nilsson to come to the house; heard from him, word for word, of Quigg's effort to corrupt him; questioned Patsy closely, getting the names of the children who had abused him; then calling Jennie into her bedroom, she locked the door behind them.

When they reëntered the sitting-room, an hour later, Jennie's lips were quivering. Tom's mouth was firmly set. Her mind was made up.

She would fight it out to the bitter end.

VI

THE BIG GRAY GOES HUNGRY

THAT invincible spirit which dwelt in Tom's breast, that spirit which had dared La-thers, outwitted Duffy, cowed Crimmins, and braved the Union, did not, strange to say, dominate all the members of her own household. One defied her. This was no other than that despoiler of new-washed clothes, old harness, wagon grease, time-books, and spring flowers, that Arab of the open lot, Stumpy the goat.

This supremacy of the goat had lasted since the eventful morning when, only a kid of tender days, he had come into the stable yard and wobbled about on his uncertain legs, nestling down near the door where Patsy lay. During all these years he had ruled over Tom. At first because his fuzzy white back and soft, silky legs had been so precious to the little cripple, and later because of his inexhaustible energy, his aggressiveness, and his marvellous activity. Brave spirits have fainted at the sight of spiders, others have turned pale at lizards, and some have shivered when cats crossed their paths. The only thing Tom feared on any number of legs, from centipedes to men, was Stumpy.

"Git out, ye imp of Satan!" she would say, raising her hand when he wandered too near, "or I'll smash ye!" The next instant she would be dodging behind the cart out of the way of Stumpy's lowered horns, with a scream as natural and as uncontrollable as that of a school-girl over a mouse. When he stood in the path cleared of snow from house to stable door, with head down, prepared to dispute every inch of the way with her, she would tramp yards around him, up to her knees in the drift, rather than face his obstinate front.

The basest of ingratitude actuated the goat. When the accident occurred that gained him his sobriquet and lost him his tail, it was Tom's quickness of hand alone that saved the remainder of his kidship from disappearing as his tail had done. Indeed, she not only choked the dog who attacked him, until he loosened his hold from want of breath, but she threw him over the stable yard fence as an additional mark of her displeasure.

In spite of her fear of him, Tom never dispossessed Stumpy. That her Patsy loved him insured him his place for life.

So Stumpy roamed through yard, kitchen, and stable, stalking over bleaching sheets, burglarizing the garden gate, and grazing wherever he chose.

The goat inspired no fear in anybody else. Jennie would chase him out of her way a dozen times a day, and Cully would play bullfight with him, and Carl and the other men would accord him his proper place, spanking him with the flat of a shovel whenever he interfered with their daily duties, or shying a corncob after him when his alertness carried him out of their reach.

This morning Jennie had missed her blue-checked apron. It had been drying on the line outside the kitchen door five minutes before. There was no one at home but herself, and she had seen nobody pass the door. Perhaps the apron had blown over into the stable yard. If it had, Carl would be sure to have seen it. She knew Carl had come home; she had been watching for him through the window. Then she ran in for her shawl.

Carl was rubbing down the Big Gray. He had been hauling ice all the morning for the brewery. The Gray was under the cart-shed, a flood of winter sunlight silvering his shaggy mane and restless ears. The Swede was scraping his sides

with the currycomb, and the Big Gray, accustomed to Cully's gentler touch, was resenting
the familiarity by biting at the tippet wound
about the neck of the young man.

Suddenly Carl raised his head — he had
caught a glimpse of a flying apron whipping
round the stable door. He knew the pattern.
It always gave him a lump in his throat, and
some little creepings down his back when he
saw it. Then he laid down the currycomb.
The next instant there came a sound as of a
barrel-head knocked in by a mixing-shovel,
and Stumpy flew through the door, followed
by Carl on the run. The familiar bit of calico
was Jennie's lost apron. One half was inside
the goat, the other half was in the hand of the
Swede.

Carl hesitated for a moment, looked cautiously about the yard, and walked slowly toward the house, his eyes on the fragments. He
never went to the house except when he was
invited, either to hear Pop read or to take his
dinner with the other men. At this instant
Jennie came running out, the shawl about her
head.

" Oh, Carl, did you find my apron ? It blew
away, and I thought it might have gone into
the yard."

73

"Yaas, mees; an' da goat see it too —
luke!" extending the tattered fragments, anger and sorrow struggling for the mastery in his
face.

"Well, I never! Carl, it was a bran'-new
one. Now just see, all the strings torn off and
the top gone! I'm just going to give Stumpy
a good beating."

Carl suggested that he run after the goat and
bring him back; but Jennie thought he was
down the road by this time, and Carl had been
working all the morning and must be tired. Besides, she must get some wood.

Carl instantly forgot the goat. He had forgotten everything, indeed, except the trim little body who stood before him looking into his
eyes. He glowed all over with inward warmth
and delight. Nobody had ever cared before
whether he was tired. When he was a little
fellow at home at Memlö his mother would
sometimes worry about his lifting the big bas-
kets of fish all day, but he could not remember
that anybody else had ever given his feelings a
thought. All this flashed through his mind as he
returned Jennie's look.

"No, no! I not tire — I brang da wood."
And then Jennie said she never meant it, and
Carl knew she did n't, of course; and then she

74

said she had never thought of such a thing, and
he agreed to that ; and they talked so long over
it, standing out in the radiance of the noonday
sun, the color coming and going in both their
faces, — Carl playing aimlessly with his tippet
tassel, and Jennie plaiting and pinching up the
ruined apron, — that the fire in the kitchen
stove went out, and the Big Gray grew hungry
and craned his long neck around the shed and
whinnied for Carl, and even Stumpy the goat
forgot his hair - breadth escape, and returned
near enough to the scene of the robbery to look
down at it from the hill above.

There is no telling how long the Big Gray
would have waited if Cully had not come home
to dinner, bringing another horse with Patsy
perched on his back. The brewery was only a
short distance, and Tom always gave her men
a hot meal at the house whenever it was possible. Had any other horse been neglected, Cully
would not have cared; but the Big Gray, which
he had driven ever since the day Tom brought
him home, — " Old Blowhard," as he would
often call him (the Gray was a bit wheezy), —
the Big Gray without his dinner !

" Hully gee ! Look at de bloke a-jollying
Jinnie, an' de Blowhard a-starvin'. Say, Patsy,"
— lifting him down, — " hold de line till I git

de Big Gray a bite. Git on ter Carl, will ye ?
I 'm a-goin' — ter — tell — de — boss,'' — with
a threatening air, weighing each word, — " jes
soon as she gits back. Ef I don't I 'm a chump.''

At sight of the boys, Jennie darted into the
house, and Carl started for the stable, his head
in the clouds, his feet on air.

" No ; I feed da horse, Cully,'' jerking at
his halter to get him away from Cully.

" A hell ov er lot ye will ! I 'll feed him meself. He 's been home an hour now, an' he ain't
half rubbed down.''

Carl made a grab for Cully, who dodged and
ran under the cart. Then a lump of ice whizzed
past Carl's ear.

" Here, stop that ! '' said Tom, entering the
gate. She had been in the city all the morning, " to look after her poor Tom,'' Pop said.
" Don't ye be throwing things round here, or
I 'll land on top of ye.''

" Well, why don't he feed de Gray, den ?
He started afore me, an' dey wants de Gray
down ter de brewery, and he up ter de house
a-buzzin' Jinnie.''

" I go brang Mees Jan's apron ; da goat eat
it oop.''

" Ye did, did ye ! What ye givin' us ? Did
n't I see ye a-chinnin' 'er whin I come over de

76

hill, — she a-leanin' up ag'in' de fence, an' youse a-talkin' ter 'er, an' ole Blowhard cryin' like his heart was broke ?"

"Eat up what apron?" asked Tom, thoroughly mystified over the situation.

"Stumpy eat da apron — I brang back da half ta Mees Jan."

" An' it took ye all the mornin' to give it to her ?" said Tom thoughtfully, looking Carl straight in the eye, a new vista opening before her.

That night when the circle gathered about the lamp to hear Pop read, Carl was missing. Tom had not sent for him.

VII

THE CONTENTS OF CULLY'S MAIL

WHEN Walking Delegate Crimmins had recovered from his amazement, after his humiliating defeat at Tom's hands, he stood irresolute for a moment outside her garden gate, indulged at some length in a form of profanity peculiar to his class, and then walked direct to McGaw's house.

That worthy Knight met him at the door. He had been waiting for him.

Young Billy McGaw also saw Crimmins enter the gate, and promptly hid himself under the broken-down steps. He hoped to overhear what was going on when the two went out again. Young Billy's inordinate curiosity was quite natural. He had heard enough of the current talk about the tenements and open lots to know that something of a revengeful and retaliatory nature against the Grogans was in the air; but as nobody who knew the exact details had confided them to him, he had determined upon an investigation of his own. He not only

78

hated Cully, but the whole Grogan household, for the pounding he had received at his hands, so he was anxious to get even in some way.

After McGaw had locked both doors, shutting out his wife and little Jack, their youngest, he took a bottle from the shelf, filled two half-tumblers, and squaring himself in his chair, said, —

"Did ye see her, Crimmy ? "

"I did," replied Crimmins, swallowing the whiskey at a gulp.

"An' she 'll come in wid us, will she ? "

"She will, will she ? She 'll come in nothin'. I jollied her about her flowers, and thought I had her dead ter rights, when she up an' asked me what we was a-goin' to do for her if she jined, an' afore I could tell her she opens the front door and gives me the dead cold."

"Fired ye ? " exclaimed McGaw incredulously.

"I 'm givin' it to ye straight, Dan; an' she pulled a gun on me, too," — telling the lie with perfect composure. "That woman 's no slouch, or I don't know 'em. One thing ye can bet yer bottom dollar on: all h—— can't scare her. We 've got to try some other way."

It was the peculiarly fertile quality of Crim-

79

mins's imagination that made him so valuable to some of his friends.

When the conspirators reached the door, neither Crimmins nor his father was in a talkative mood, and Billy heard nothing. They lingered a moment on the sill, within a foot of his head as he lay in a cramped position below, and then they sauntered out, his father bareheaded, to the stable yard. There McGaw leaned upon a cart wheel, listening dejectedly to Crimmins, who seemed to be outlining a plan of some kind, which at intervals lightened the gloom of McGaw's despair, judging from the expression of his father's face. Then he turned hurriedly to the house, cursed his wife because he could not find his big fur cap, and started across to the village. Billy followed, keeping a safe distance behind.

Tom, after Patsy's sad experience, forbade him the streets, and never allowed him out of her sight unless Cully or her father were with him. She knew a storm was gathering, and she was watching the clouds and waiting for the first patter of rain. When it came she intended that every one of her people should be under cover. She had sent for Carl and her two stablemen, and told them that if they were dissatisfied in any way she wanted to know it at once. If the wages she was paying were not enough, she was willing to raise them, but she wanted them distinctly to understand that as she had built up the business herself, she was the only one who had a right to manage it, adding that she would rather clean and drive the horses herself than be dictated to by any person outside. She said that she saw trouble brewing, and knew that her men would feel it first. They must look out for themselves coming home late at night. At the brewery strike, two years before, hardly a day had passed that some of the non-union men were not beaten into insensibility.

That night Carl came back again to the porch door, and in his quiet, earnest way said, " We have t'ink 'bout da Union. Da men not go — not laik da Union man. We not 'fraid," tapping his hip pocket, where, sailor-like, he always carried his knife sheathed in a leather case.

Tom's eyes kindled as she looked into his manly face. She loved pluck and grit. She knew the color of the blood running in this young fellow's veins.

Week after week passed, and though now and then she caught the mutterings of distant thunder, as Cully or some of the others overheard a remark on the ferry-boat or about the post-office, no other signs of the threatened storm were visible.

Then it broke.

One morning an important-looking envelope lay in her letter-box. It was long and puffy, and was stamped in the upper corner with a picture of a brewery in full operation. One end bore an inscription addressed to the postmaster, stating that in case Mr. Thomas Grogan was not found within ten days, it should be returned to Schwartz & Co., Brewers.

The village post-office had several other letter-boxes, faced with glass, so that the contents of each could be seen from the outside. Two of these contained similar envelopes, looking equally important, one being addressed to Mc-Gaw.

When he had called for his mail, the close resemblance between the two envelopes seen in the letter-boxes set McGaw to thinking. Actual scrutiny through the glass revealed the picture of the brewery on each. He knew then that Tom had been asked to bid for the brewery hauling. That night a special meeting of the Union was called at eight o'clock. Quigg, Crimmins, and McGaw signed the call.

" Hully gee, what a wad! " said Cully, when

the postmaster passed Tom's big letter out to him. One of Cully's duties was to go for the mail.

When Pop broke the seal in Tom's presence, — one of Pop's duties was to open what Cully brought, — out dropped a typewritten sheet notifying Mr. Thomas Grogan that sealed proposals would be received up to March 1 for "unloading, hauling, and delivering to the bins of the Eagle Brewery" so many tons of coal and malt, together with such supplies, etc. There were also blank forms in duplicate to be duly filled up with the price and signature of the bidder. This contract was given out once a year. Twice before it had been awarded to Thomas Grogan. The year before a man from Stapleton had bid lowest, and had done the work. Mc-Gaw and his friends complained that it took the bread out of Rockville's mouth; but as the bidder belonged to the Union, no protest could be made.

The morning after the meeting of the Union, McGaw went to New York by the early boat. He carried a letter from Pete Lathers, the yard-master, to Crane & Co., of so potent a character that the coal dealers agreed to lend McGaw five hundred dollars on his three months' note, taking a chattel mortgage on his teams and carts as security, the money to be paid McGaw as soon as the papers were drawn. McGaw, in return, was to use his "pull" to get a permit from the village trustees for the free use of the village dock by Crane & Co. for discharging their Rockville coal. This would save Crane half a mile to haul. It was this promise made by McGaw which really turned the scale in his favor. To hustle successfully it was often necessary for Crane to cut some sharp corners.

This dock, as McGaw knew perfectly well, had been leased to another party — the Fertilizing Company — for two years, and could not possibly be placed at Crane's disposal. But he said nothing of this to Crane.

When the day of payment to McGaw arrived, Dempsey of the executive committee and Walking Delegate Quigg met McGaw at the ferry on his return from New York. McGaw had Crane's money in his pocket. That night he paid two hundred dollars into the Union, two hundred to his feed-man on an account long overdue, and the balance to Quigg in a poker game in the back room over O'Leary's bar.

Tom also had an interview with Mr. Crane shortly after his interview with McGaw. Something she said about the dock having been leased to the Fertilizing Company caused Crane to

84

leave his chair in a hurry, and ask his clerk in an angry voice if McGaw had yet been paid the money on his chattel mortgage. When his cashier showed him the stub of the check, dated two days before, Crane slammed the door behind him, his teeth set tight, little puffs of profanity escaping between the openings. As he walked with Tom to the door, he said, —

"Send your papers up, Tom. I'll go bond any day in the year for you, and for any amount ; but I'll get even with McGaw for that lie he told me about the dock, if it takes my bank account."

The annual hauling contract for the brewery, which had become an important one in Rockville, its business having nearly doubled in the last few years, was of special value to Tom at this time, and she determined to make every effort to secure it.

Pop filled up the proposal in his round, clear hand, and Tom signed it, " Thomas Grogan, Rockville, Staten Island." Then Pop witnessed it, and Mr. Crane, a few days later, duly inscribed the firm's name under the clause reserved for bondsmen. After that Tom brought the bid home, and laid it on the shelf over her bed.

Everything was now ready for the fight.

The bids were to be opened at noon in the office of the brewery.

By eleven o'clock the hangers-on and idlers began to lounge into the big yard paved with cobblestones. At half past eleven McGaw got out of a buggy, accompanied by Quigg. At a quarter to twelve Tom, in her hood and ulster, walked rapidly through the gate, and, without as much as a look at the men gathered about the office door, pushed her way into the room. Then she picked up a chair, and placing it against the wall, sat down. Sticking out of the breast pocket of her ulster was the big envelope containing her bid.

Five minutes before the hour the men began filing in one by one, awkwardly uncovering their heads, and standing in one another's way. Some, using their hats as screens, looked over the rims. When the bids were being gathered up by the clerk, Dennis Quigg handed over McGaw's. The ease with which Dan had raised the money on his notes had invested that gentleman with some of the dignity and attributes of a capitalist: the hired buggy and the obsequious Quigg indicated this. His new position was strengthened by the liberal way in which he had portioned out his possessions to the workingman. It was further sustained by the

86

hope that he might perhaps repeat his generosi-
ties in the near future.

At twelve o'clock precisely Mr. Schwartz, a
round, bullet-headed German, entered the room,
turned his revolving chair, and began to cut the
six envelopes heaped up before him on his desk,
reading the prices aloud as he opened them in
succession, the clerk recording. The first four
were from parties in outside villages. Then
came McGaw's: "Forty-nine cents for coal,
etc."

So far he was lowest. Quigg twisted his hat
nervously, and McGaw's coarse face grew red
and white by turns.

Tom's bid was the last. "Thomas Grogan,
Rockville, Staten Island, thirty-eight cents for
coal, etc."

"Gentlemen," said Mr. Schwartz quietly,
"Thomas Grogan gets the hauling."

VIII

POP MULLINS'S ADVICE

ALMOST every man and woman in the tenement district knew Oscar Schwartz, and had felt the power of his obstinate hand during the long strike of two years before, when, the Union having declared war, Schwartz had closed the brewery for several months rather than submit to its dictation. The news, therefore, that the Union had called a meeting and appointed a committee to wait on Mr. Schwartz, to protest against his giving work to a non-union woman, filled them with alarm. The women remembered the privations and suffering of that winter, and the three dollars a week doled out to them by the Central Branch, while their husbands, who had been earning two and three dollars a day, were drinking at O'Leary's bar, playing cards, or listening to the encouraging talk of the delegates who came from New York to keep up their spirits. The brewery employed a larger number of men than any other concern in Rockville, so trouble with its employees

88

meant serious trouble for half the village if
Schwartz defied the Union and selected a non-
union woman to do the work.

They knew, too, something of the indomitable pluck and endurance of Tom Grogan. If she
were lowest on the bids, she would fight for the
contract, they felt sure, if it took her last dollar.
McGaw was a fool, they said, to bid so high ;
he might have known she would cut his throat,
and bring them no end of trouble.

Having nursed their resentment, and needing
a common object for their wrath, the women
broke out against Tom. Many of them had dis-
liked her ever since the day, years ago, when
she had been seen carrying her injured husband
away at night to the hospital, after months of
nursing at home. And the most envious had
always maintained that she meant at the time
to put him away forever where no one could
find him, so that she might play the man herself.

"Why should she be a-comin' in an' a-rob-
bin' us of our pay ? " muttered a coarse, red-
faced virago, her hair in a frowze about her
head, her slatternly dress open at the throat.
" Oi 'll be one to go an' pull her off the dock
and jump on her. What 's she a-doin', anyhow, puttin' down prices ? Ef her ole man had

a leg to walk on, instid of his lyin' to-day a cripple in the hospital, he 'd be back and be a-runnin' things.''

"She 's doin' what she 's a right to do," broke out Mrs. Todd indignantly. Mrs. Todd was the wife of the foreman at the brewery, and an old friend of Tom's. Tom had sat up with her child only the week before. Indeed, there were few women in the tenements, for all their outcry, who did not know how quick had been her hand to help when illness came, or the landlord threatened the sidewalk, or the undertaker insisted on his money in advance.

"It 's not Tom Grogan that 's crooked," Mrs. Todd continued, "an' ye all know it. It 's that loafer, Dennis Quigg, and that old sneak, Crimmins. They never lifted their hands on a decent job in their lives, an' don't want to. When my man Jack was out of work for four months last winter, and there was n't a pail of coal in the house, was n't Quigg gittin' his four dollars a day for shootin' off his mouth every night at O'Leary's, an' fillin' the men's heads full of capital and rights ? An' Dan McGaw 's no better. If ye 're out for jumpin' on people, Mrs. Moriarty, begin with Quigg an' some of the bummers as is runnin' the Union, an' as gits paid whether the men works or not."

"Bedad, ye 're roight," said half a dozen women, the tide turning suddenly, while the excitement grew and spread, and other women came in from the several smaller tenements.

"Is the trouble at the brewery ? " asked a shrunken-looking woman, opening a door on the corridor, a faded shawl over her head. She was a newcomer, and had been in the tenement only a week or so, — not long enough to have the run of the house or to know her neighbors.

"Yes ; at Schwartz's," said Mrs. Todd, stopping opposite the speaker's door on the way to her own rooms. "Your man 's got a job there, ain't he ? "

"He has, mum, — he 's gateman, the fust job in six months. Ye don't think they 'll make him throw it up, do ye, mum ? "

"Yes ; an' break his head if he don't. That 's what they did to my man three years gone, till he had to come in with the gang and pay 'em two dollars a month," replied Mrs. Todd.

"But my man 's jined, mum, a month ago ; they would n't let him work till he did. Won't ye come in an' set down ? It 's a poor place we have, — we 've been so long without work, an' my girl 's laid off with a cough. She 's been a-workin' at the box factory. If the Union give notice again, I don't know what 'll become of us. Can't we do somethin' ? Maybe Mrs. Grogan might give up the work if she knew how it was wid us. She seems like a dacent woman; she was in to look at me girl last week, hearin' as how we were strangers an' she very bad."

"Oh, ye don't know her. Ye can save yer wind and shoe leather. She 's on ter McGaw red hot; that 's the worst of it. He better look out; she 'll down him yet," said Mrs. Todd.

As the two entered the stuffy, close room for further discussion, a young girl left her seat by the window, and moved into the adjoining apartment. She had that yellow, waxy skin, hollow, burning eyes, and hectic flush which tell the fatal story so clearly.

While the women of the tenements were cursing or wringing their hands, the men were devoting themselves to more vigorous measures. A meeting was called for nine o'clock at Lion Hall.

It was held behind closed doors. Two walking delegates from Brooklyn were present, — having been summoned by telegram the night before. They were expected to coax or bully the weak-kneed, should the ultimatum sent to Schwartz be refused and an order for a sympathetic strike issued.

At the brewery all was quiet. Schwartz had read the notice left on his desk by the committee the night before, and had already begun his arrangements to supply the places of the men if a strike were ordered. When pressed by Quigg for a reply, he said quietly, —

"The price for hauling will be Grogan's bid. If she wants it, it is hers."

Tom talked the matter over with Pop, and had determined to buy another horse and hire two extra carts. At her price there was a margin of at least ten cents a ton profit, and as the work lasted through the year, she could adjust the hauling of her other business, without much extra expense. She discussed the situation with no one outside her house. If Schwartz wanted her to carry on the work, she would do it, Union or no Union. Mr. Crane was on her bond. That in itself was a bracing factor. Strong and self-reliant as she was, the helping hand which this man held out to her was like an anchor in a storm.

That Sunday night they were all gathered round the kerosene lamp, — Pop reading, Cully and Patsy on the floor, Jennie listening absent-mindedly, her thoughts far away, — when there came a knock at the kitchen door. Jennie flew to open it.

Outside stood two women. One was Mrs. Todd, the other the haggard, pinched, careworn woman who had spoken to her that morning at her room door in the tenement.

"They want to see you, mother," said Jennie, all the light gone out of her eyes. What could be the matter with Carl, she thought. It had been this way for a week.

"Well, bring 'em in. Hold on, I'll go meself."

"She *would* come, Tom," said Mrs. Todd, unwinding her shawl from her head and shoulders; "an' ye must n't blame me, fer it 's none of my doin's. Walk in, mum; ye can speak to her yerself. Why, where is she?" looking out of the door into the darkness. "Oh, here ye are; I thought ye 'd skipped."

"Do ye remember me?" said the woman, stepping into the room, her gaunt face looking more wretched under the flickering light of the candle than it had done in the morning. "I 'm the newcomer in the tenements. Ye were in to see my girl th' other night. We 're in great trouble."

"She 's not dead?" said Tom, sinking into a chair.

"No, thank God; we 've got her still wid us; but me man 's come home to-night nigh

94

crazy. He 's a-walkin' the floor this minute, an' so I goes to Mrs. Todd, an' she come wid me. If he loses the job now, we 're in the street. Only two weeks' work since las' fall, an' the girl gettin' worse every day, and every cint in the bank gone, an' hardly a chair lef' in the place. An' I says to him, 'I'll go meself. She come in to see Katie th' other night; she 'll listen to me.' We lived in Newark, mum, an' had four rooms and a mahogany sofa and two carpets, till the strike come in the clock factory, an' me man had to quit; an' then all winter — oh, we 're not used to the likes of this!'" and she covered her face with her shawl and burst into tears.

Tom had risen to her feet, her face expressing the deepest sympathy for the woman, though she was at a loss to understand the cause of her visitor's distress.

"Is yer man fired?" she asked.

"No, an' would n't be if they'd let him alone. He 's sober an' steady, an' never tastes a drop, and brings his money home to me every Saturday night, and always done; an' now they" —

"Well, what 's the matter, then?" Tom could not stand much beating about the bush.

"Why, don't ye know they've give notice?"

she said in astonishment; then, as a misgiving entered her mind, "Maybe I 'm wrong; but me man an' all of 'em tells me ye 're a-buckin' ag'in' Mr. McGaw, an' that ye has the haulin' job at the brewery."

"No," said Tom, with emphasis, "ye 're not wrong; ye 're dead right. But who 's give notice?"

"The committee 's give notice, an' the boss at the brewery says he 'll give ye the job if he has to shut up the brewery; an' the committee 's decided to-day that if he does they 'll call out the men. My man is a member, and so I come over" — And she rested her head wearily against the door, the tears streaming down her face.

Tom looked at her wonderingly, and then, putting her strong arms about her, half carried her across the kitchen to a chair by the stove. Mrs. Todd leaned against the table, watching the sobbing woman.

For a moment no one spoke. It was a new experience for Tom. Heretofore the fight had been her own and for her own. She had never supposed before that she filled so important a place in the neighborhood, and for a moment there flashed across her mind a certain justifiable pride in the situation. But this feeling was momentary. Here was a suffering woman. For the first time she realized that one weaker than herself might suffer in the struggle. What could she do to help her? This thought was uppermost in her mind.

" Don't ye worry," she said tenderly. "Schwartz won't fire yer man."

" No; but the sluggers will. There was five men 'p'inted to-day to do up the scabs an' the kickers who won't go out. They near killed him once in Newark for kickin'. It was that time, you know, when Katie was first took bad."

" Do ye know their names?" said Tom, her eyes flashing.

" No, an' me man don't. He's new, an' they dar's n't trust him. It was in the back room, he says, that they picked 'em out."

Tom stood for some moments in deep thought, gazing at the fire, her arms akimbo. Then, wheeling suddenly, she opened the door of the sitting-room, and said in a firm, resolute voice,—

" Gran'pop, come here; I want ye!"

The old man laid down his book, and stood in the kitchen doorway. He was in his shirt-sleeves, his spectacles on his forehead.

" Come inside the kitchen, an' shut that door behind ye. Here's me friend Jane Todd an' a friend of hers from the tenement. That thief

97

of a McGaw has stirred up the Union over the haulin' bid, and they've sent notice to Schwartz that I don't belong to the Union, an' if he don't throw me over an' give the job to McGaw they'll call out the men. If they do, there's a hundred women and three times that many children that'll go hungry. This woman here's got a girl herself that has n't drawed a well breath for six months, an' her man's been idle all winter, an' only just now got a job at Schwartz's, tending gate. Now, what'll I do? Shall I chuck up the job or stick?"

The old man looked into the desolate, weary face of the woman and then at Tom. Then he said slowly, —

"Well, child, ye kin do widout it, an' maybe t' others can't."

"Ye 've got it straight," said Tom; "that's just what I think meself." Then turning to the stranger, —

"Go home and tell yer man to go to bed. I'll touch nothin' that'll break the heart of any woman. The job's McGaw's. I'll throw up me bid."

IX

WHAT A SPARROW SAW

EVER since the eventful morning when Carl had neglected the Big Gray for a stolen hour with Jennie, Cully had busied himself in devising ways of making the Swede's life miserable. With a boy's keen insight, he had discovered enough to convince him that Carl was "dead mashed on Jennie," as he put it, but whether "for keeps" or not, he had not yet determined. He had already enriched his songs with certain tender allusions to their present frame of mind and their future state of happiness. "Where was Moses when the light went out?" and "Little Annie Rooney" had undergone so subtle a change when sung at the top of Mr. James Finnegan's voice, that while the original warp and woof of those very popular melodies were entirely unrecognizable to any but the persons interested, to them they were as gall and wormwood. This was Cully's invariable way of expressing his opinions on current affairs. He would sit on the front board of his

99

cart, — the Big Gray stumbling over the stones as he walked, the reins lying loose, — and fill the air with details of events passing in the village, with all the gusto of a variety actor. The impending strike at the brewery had been made the basis of a paraphrase of "Johnnie, get your gun;" and even McGaw's red head had come in for its share of abuse to the air of "Fire, boys, fire!" So for a time this new development of tenderness on the part of Carl for Jennie served to ring the changes on "Moses" and "Annie Rooney."

Carl's budding hopes had been slightly nipped by the cold look in Tom's eye when she asked him if it took an hour to give Jennie a tattered apron. With some disappointment he noticed that except at rare intervals, and then only when Tom was at home, he was no longer invited to the house. He had always been a timid, shrinking fellow where a woman was concerned, having followed the sea and lived among men since he was sixteen years old. During these earlier years he had made two voyages in the Pacific, and another to the whaling-ground in the Arctic seas. On this last voyage, in a gale of wind, he had saved all the lives aboard a brig, the crew helpless from scurvy. When the lifeboat reached the lee of her stern, Carl, at the risk of his life, climbed aboard, caught a line, and lowered the men, one by one, into the rescuing yawl. He could with perfect equanimity have faced another storm and rescued a second crew any hour of the day or night, but he could not face a woman's displeasure. Moreover, what Tom wanted done was law to Carl. She had taken him out of the streets and given him a home. He would serve her in whatever way she wished as long as he lived.

He and Gran'pop were fast friends. On rainy days, or when work was dull in the winter months, the old man would often come into Carl's little chamber, next the harness-room in the stable, and sit on his bed by the hour. And Carl would tell him about his people at home, and show him the pictures tacked over his bed, those of his old mother with her white cap and of the young sister who was soon to be married.

On Sundays Carl followed Tom and her family to church, waiting until they had left the house. He always sat far back near the door, so that he could see them come out. Then he would overtake Pop with Patsy, whenever the little fellow could go. This was not often, for now there were many days when the boy had to lie all day on the lounge in the sitting-room,

poring over his books, or playing with Stumpy,
brought into the kitchen to amuse him.

Since the day of Tom's warning look, Carl
rarely joined her daughter. Jennie would loiter
by the way, speaking to the girls, but he would
hang back. He felt that Tom did not want them
together.

One spring morning, however, a new com-
plication arose. It was a morning when the
sky was a delicate violet blue, when the sunlight came tempered through a tender land haze
and a filmy mist from the still sea, when all
the air was redolent with sweet smells of coming spring, and all the girls were gay in new
attire. Dennis Quigg had been lounging outside the church door, his silk hat and green
satin necktie glistening in the sun. When Jennie tripped out Quigg started forward. The
look on his face, as with swinging shoulders he
slouched beside her, sent a thrill of indignation
through Carl. He could give her up, perhaps,
if Tom insisted, but never to a man like Quigg.
Before the walking delegate had "passed the
time of day," the young sailor was close beside
Jennie, within touch of her hand.

There was no love lost between the two men.
Carl had not forgotten the proposition Quigg
had made to him to leave Tom's employ, nor

had Quigg forgotten the uplifted shovel with
which his proposal had been greeted. Yet there
was no well-defined jealousy between them.
Mr. Walking Delegate Dennis Quigg, confidential agent of Branch No. 3, Knights of Labor,
had too good an opinion of himself ever to look
upon that " tow-headed duffer of a stableboy "
in the light of a rival. Nor could Carl for a
moment think of that narrow-chested, red-faced,
flashily dressed Knight as being able to make
the slightest impression on " Mees Jan."

Quigg, however, was more than welcome to
Jennie to-day. A little sense of wounded pride
sent the hot color to her cheeks when she thought
of Carl's apparent neglect. He had hardly spoken
to her in weeks. What had she done that he
should treat her so ? She would show him that
there were just as good fellows about as Mr.
Carl Nilsson.

But all this faded out when Carl joined her,
— Carl, so straight, clear-skinned, brown, and
ruddy; his teeth so white, his eyes so blue !
She could see out of the corner of her eye how
the hair curled in tiny rings on his temples.

Still it was to Quigg she talked. And more
than that, she gave him her prayer-book to
carry until she fixed her glove, the glove that
needed no fixing at all. And she chattered on

about the dance at the boat club, and the pic-
nic which was to come off when the weather
grew warmer.

And Carl walked silent beside her, with his
head up and his heart down, and the tears very
near his eyes.

When they reached the outer gate of the
stable yard, and Quigg had slouched off without even raising his hat, — the absence of all
courtesy stands in a certain class for a mark of
higher respect, — Carl swung back the gate,
and held it open for her to pass in. Jennie loitered for a moment. There was a look in Carl's
face she had not seen before. She had not
meant to hurt him, she said to herself.

"What mak' you no lak me anna more,
Mees Jan? I big annough to carry da buke,"
said Carl.

"Why, how you talk, Carl! I never said
such a word," answered Jennie, leaning over
the fence, her heart fluttering.

The air was soft as a caress. Opal - tinted
clouds with violet shadows sailed above the
low hills. In the shade of the fence dandelions
had burst into bloom. From a bush near by a
song-sparrow flung a note of spring across the
meadow.

"Well, you nev' cam' to stable anna more,

Mees Jan,'' Carl said slowly, in a tender, pleading tone, his gaze on her face.

The girl reached through the fence for the
golden flower. She dared not trust herself to
look. She knew what was in her lover's eyes.

"I get ta flower," said Carl, vaulting the
fence with one hand.

"No; please don't trouble. Oh, Carl!"
she exclaimed suddenly. "The horrid brier!
My hand's all scratched!"

"Ah, Mees Jan, I so sorry! Let Carl see it,"
he said, his voice melting. "I tak' ta brier out,"
pushing back the tangled vines of last year to
bring himself nearer.

The clouds sailed on. The sparrow stood on
its tallest toes and twisted its little neck.

"Oh, please do, Carl, it hurts so!" she
said, laying her little round hand in the big,
strong, horny palm that had held the life-line
the night of the wreck.

The song-sparrow clung to the swaying top
of a mullein-stalk near by, and poured out a
strong, swelling, joyous song that wellnigh
split its throat.

When Tom called Jennie, half an hour later,
she and Carl were still talking across the fence.

X

CULLY WINS BY A NECK

ABOUT this time the labor element in the
village and vicinity was startled by an
advertisement in the Rockville "Daily News,"
signed by the clerk of the Board of Village Trustees, notifying contractors that thirty days
thereafter, closing at nine P. M. precisely, sepa-
rate sealed proposals would be received at the
meeting room of the board, over the post-
office, for the hauling of twenty thousand cu-
bic yards of fine crushed stone for use on the
public highways ; bidders would be obliged to
give suitable bonds, etc., — certified check for
five hundred dollars to accompany each bid as
guarantee, etc.

The news was a grateful surprise to the workingmen. The hauling and placing of so large an
amount of material as soon as spring opened
meant plenty of work for many shovellers and
pickers. The local politicians, of course, had
known all about it for weeks ; especially those
who owned property fronting on the streets to be

improved ; they had helped the appropriation through the finance committee. McGaw, too, had known about it from the first day of its discussion before the board. Those who were inside the ring had decided then that he would be the best man to haul the stone. The "steal," they knew, could best be arranged in the tally of the carts, the final check on the scow measurement. They knew too that McGaw's accounts could be controlled, and the total result easily "fixed." The stone itself had been purchased of the manufacturers the year before, but there were not funds enough to put it on the roads at that time.

Here, then, was McGaw's chance. His triumph at obtaining the brewery contract had been but short-lived. Schwartz had given him the work, but at Tom's price, not at his own. McGaw had accepted it, hoping for profits that would help him with his chattel mortgage. After he had been at work for a month, however, he found that he ran behind. He began to see that, in spite of its boastings, the Union had really done nothing for him, except indirectly with its threatened strike. The Union, on the other hand, insisted that it had been McGaw's business to arrange his own terms with Schwartz. What it had done was to kill Grogan as a competitor, and knock her non-union men out of the job. This ended its duty.

While the leaders said this much to McGaw, so far as outsiders could know, they claimed that the Union had scored a brilliant victory. The Brooklyn and New York branches duly paraded it as another triumph over capital, and their bank accounts were accordingly increased with new dues and collections.

With this new contract in his possession, McGaw felt certain he could cancel his debt with Crane and get even with the world. He began his arrangements at once. Police-Justice Rowan, the prospective candidate for the Assembly, who had acquired some landed property by the purchase of expired tax titles, agreed to furnish the certified check for five hundred dollars and to sign McGaw's bond for a consideration to be subsequently agreed upon. A brother of Rowan's, a contractor, who was finishing some grading at Quarantine Landing, had also consented, for a consideration, to loan McGaw what extra teams he required.

The size of the contract was so great, and the deposit check and bond were so large, that McGaw concluded at once that the competition would be narrowed down between himself and Rowan's brother, with Justice Rowan as backer, and perhaps one other firm from across the island, near New Brighton. His own advantage over other bidders was in his living on the spot, with his stables and teams near at hand.

Tom, he felt assured, was out of the way. Not only was the contract very much too large for her, requiring twice as many carts as she possessed, but now that the spring work was about to begin, and Babcock's sea wall work to be resumed, she had all the stevedoring she could do for her own customers, without going outside for additional business.

Moreover, she had apparently given up the fight, for she had bid on no work of any kind since the morning she had called upon Schwartz and told him, in her blunt, frank way, "Give the work to McGaw at me price. It's enough and fair."

Tom, meanwhile, made frequent visits to New York, returning late at night. One day she brought home a circular with cuts of several improved kinds of hoisting-engines with automatic dumping-buckets. She showed them to Pop under the kerosene lamp at night, explaining to him their advantages in handling small material like coal or broken stone. Once she so far relaxed her rules in regard to Jennie's lover as to send for Carl to come to the house after supper, questioning him closely about the upper rigging of a new derrick she had seen. Carl's experience as a sailor was especially valuable in matters of this kind. He could not only splice a broken "fall," and repair the sheaves and friction-rollers in a hoisting-block, but whenever the rigging got tangled aloft he could spring up the derrick like a cat and unreeve the rope in an instant. She also wrote to Babcock, asking him to stop at her house some morning on his way to the Quarantine Landing, where he was building a retaining-wall; and when he arrived, she took him out to the shed where she kept her heavy derricks. That more experienced contractor at once became deeply interested, and made a series of sketches for her, on the back of an envelope, of an improved pintle and revolving-cap which he claimed would greatly improve the working of her derricks. These sketches she took to the village blacksmith next day, and by that night had an estimate of their cost. She was also seen one morning, when the new trolley company got rid of its old stock, at a sale of car-horses, watching the prices closely, and examining the condition of the animals sold. She asked the superintendent to drop her a postal when the next sale occurred. To her neighbors, however,

and even to her own men, she said nothing.
The only man in the village to whom she had
spoken regarding the new work was the clerk
of the board, and then only casually as to the
exact time when the bids would be received.

The day before the eventful night when the
proposals were to be opened, Mr. Crane, in his
buggy, stopped at her house on his way back
from the fort, and they drove together to the
ferry. When she returned she called Pop into
the kitchen, shut the door, and showed him the
bid duly signed and a slip of pink paper. This
was a check of Crane & Co.'s to be deposited
with the bid. Then she went down to the stable and had a long conference with Cully.

The Board of Village Trustees consisted of
nine men, representing a fair average of the
intelligence and honesty of the people. The
president was a reputable hardware merchant,
a very good citizen, who kept a store largely
patronized by local contractors. The other members were two lawyers, — young men working
up in practice with the assistance of a political
pull, — a veterinary surgeon, and five gentlemen
of leisure, whose only visible means of support
were derived from pool rooms and ward meet-
ings. Every man on the board, except the surgeon and the president, had some particular

axe to grind. One wished to be sheriff; another, county clerk. The five gentlemen of leisure wished to stay where they were. When a pie was cut, these five held the knife. It was their fault, they said, when they went hungry.

In the side of this body politic the surgeon was a thorn as sharp as any one of his scalpels. He was a hard-headed, sober-minded Scotchman, who had been elected to represent a group of his countrymen living in the eastern part of the village, and whose profession, the five supposed, indicated without doubt his entire willingness to see through a cart wheel, especially when the hub was silver-plated. At the first meeting of the board they learned their mistake, but it did not worry them much. They had seven votes to two.

The council-chamber of the board was a hall — large for Rockville — situated over the post-office, and only two doors from O'Leary's barroom. It was the ordinary village hall, used for everything from a Christmas festival to a prize-fight. In summer it answered for a skating rink.

Once a month the board occupied it. On these occasions a sort of rostrum was brought in for the president, besides a square table and a dozen chairs. These were placed at one end, and were partitioned off by a wooden rail to form an inclosure, outside of which always stood the citizens. On the wall hung a big eight-day clock. Over the table, about which were placed chairs, a kerosene lamp swung on a brass chain. Opposite each seat lay a square of blotting-paper and some cheap pens and paper. Down the middle of the table were three inkstands, standing in china plates.

The board always met in the evening, as the business hours of the members prevented their giving the day to their deliberations.

Upon the night of the letting of the contract the first man to arrive was McGaw. He ran up the stairs hurriedly, found no one he was looking for, and returned to O'Leary's, where he was joined by Justice Rowan and his brother John, the contractor, Quigg, Crimmins, and two friends of the Union. During the last week the Union had been outspoken in its aid of Mc-Gaw, and its men had quietly passed the word of "Hands off this job!" about in the neighborhood. If McGaw got the work — and there was now not the slightest doubt of it — he would, of course, employ all Union men. If anybody else got it — well, they would attend to him later. "One thing was certain: no ' scab ' from

113

New Brighton should come over and take it."
They'd do up anybody who tried that game.

When McGaw, surrounded by his friends,
entered the board-room again, the place was
full. Outside the rail stood a solid mass of people. Inside, every seat was occupied. It was
too important a meeting for any trustee to miss.

McGaw stood on his toes and looked over
the heads. To his delight, Tom was not in the
room, and no one representing her. If he had
had any lingering suspicion of her bidding, her
non-appearance allayed it. He knew now that
she was out of the race. Moreover, no New
Brighton people had come. He whispered this
information to Justice Rowan's brother behind
his big, speckled hand covered with its red, spidery hair. Then the two forced their way out
again, entered the post-office, and borrowed a
pen. Once there, McGaw took from his side
pocket two large envelopes, the contents of
which he spread out under the light.

"I'm dead roight," said McGaw. "I'll put
up the price of this other bid. There ain't a
man round here that dares show his head. The
Union's fixed 'em."

"Will the woman bid?" asked his companion.

"The woman! What'd she be a-doin' wid

a bid loike that ? She c'u'd n't handle the half
of it. I 'll wait till a few minutes to nine o'clock.
Ye kin fix up both these bids an' hold 'em in
yer pocket. Thin we kin see what bids is laid
on the table. Ours 'll go in last. If there 's
nothin' else we 'll give 'em the high one. I 'll
git inside the rail, so 's to be near the table.''

When the two squeezed back through the
throng again into the board-room, even the
staircase was packed. McGaw pulled off his
fur cap and struggled past the rail, bowing to
the president. The justice's brother stood outside, within reach of McGaw's hand. McGaw
glanced at the clock and winked complacently
at his prospective partner, — not a single bid had
been handed in. Then he thrust out his long
arm, took from Rowan's brother the big envelope containing the higher bid, and dropped it
on the table.

Just then there was a commotion at the door.
Somebody was trying to force a passage in. The
president rose from his chair, and looked over
the crowd. McGaw started from his chair,
looked anxiously at the clock, then at his partner. The body of a boy struggling like an eel
worked its way through the mass, dodged under
the wooden bar, and threw an envelope on the
table.

"Dat 's Tom Grogan's bid," he said, looking at the president. "Hully gee! but dat was
a close shave! She telled me not ter dump it
till one minute o' nine, an' de bloke at de door
come near sp'ilin' de game till I give him one
in de mug."

At this instant the clock struck nine, and the
president's gavel fell.

"Time 's up," said the Scotchman.

XI

A TWO-DOLLAR BILL

THE excitement over the outcome of the bidding was intense. The barroom at O'Leary's was filled with a motley crowd of men, most of whom belonged to the Union, and all of whom had hoped to profit in some way had the contract fallen into the hands of the political ring who were dominating the affairs of the village. The more hot-headed and out-spoken swore vengeance, not only against the horse doctor, who had refused to permit McGaw to smuggle in the second bid, but against Crane & Co. and everybody else who had helped to defeat their schemes. They meant to boycott Crane before to-morrow night. He should not unload or freight another cargo of coal until they allowed it. The village powers, they admitted, could not be boycotted, but they would do everything they could to make it uncomfortable for the board if it awarded the contract to Grogan. Neither would they forget the trustees at the next election. As to that "smart Alec"

of a horse doctor, they knew how to fix him.
Suppose it had struck nine and the polls had
closed, what right had he to keep McGaw from
handing in his other bid? (Both were higher
than Tom's. This fact, however, McGaw had
never mentioned.)

Around the tenements the interest was no
less marked. Mr. Moriarty had sent the news
of Tom's success ringing through O'Leary's,
and Mrs. Moriarty, waiting outside the barroom
door for the pitcher her husband had filled for
her inside, had spread its details through every
hallway in the tenement.

" Ah, but Tom 's a keener," said that gossip.
"Think of that little divil Cully jammed behind the door with her bid in his hand a-waitin'
for the clock to get round to two minutes o'
nine, an' that big stuff Dan McGaw sittin' inside wid *two* bids up his sleeve ! Oh, but she 's
cunnin', she is ! Dan 's clean beat. He 'll niver
haul a shovel o' that stone."

"How 'll she be a-doin' a job like that ?"
came from a woman listening over the banisters.

" Be doin' ?" rejoined a red-headed virago.
"Would n't ye be doin' it yerself if ye had that
big coal dealer behind ye ?"

"Oh, we hear enough. Who says they 're
in it ?" rejoined a third listener.

"Pete Lathers says so, the yard boss. He was a-tellin' me man yisterday."

On consulting Justice Rowan the next morning, McGaw and his friends found but little comfort. The law was explicit, the justice said. The contract must be given to the lowest responsible bidder. Tom had deposited her certified check of five hundred dollars with the bid, and there was no informality in her proposal. He was sorry for McGaw, but if Mrs. Grogan signed the contract there was no hope for him. The horse doctor's action was right. If McGaw's second bid had been received, it would simply have invalidated both of his, the law forbidding two from the same bidder.

Rowan's opinion sustaining Tom's right was a blow he did not expect. Furthermore, the justice offered no hope for the future. The law gave Tom the award, and nothing could prevent her hauling the stone if she signed the contract. These words rang in McGaw's ears — *if she signed the contract*. On this *if* hung his only hope.

Rowan was too shrewd a politician, now that McGaw's chances were gone, to advise any departure, even by a hair-line, from the strict letter of the law. He was, moreover, too upright as a justice to advise any member of the defeated party to an overt act which might look like unfairness to any bidder concerned. He had had a talk, besides, with his brother over night, and they had accordingly determined to watch events. Should a way be found of rejecting on legal grounds Tom's bid, making a new advertisement necessary, Rowan meant to ignore McGaw altogether, and have his brother bid in his own name. This determination was strengthened when McGaw, in a burst of confidence, told Rowan of his present financial straits.

From Rowan's the complaining trio adjourned to O'Leary's barroom. Crimmins and McGaw entered first. Quigg arrived later. He closed one eye meaningly as he entered, and O'Leary handed a brass key to him over the bar with the remark, " Stamp on the floor three toimes, Dinny, an' I'll send yez up what ye want to drink." Then Crimmins opened a door concealed by a wooden screen, and the three disappeared upstairs. Crimmins reappeared within an hour, and hurried out the front door. In a few moments he returned with Justice Rowan, who had adjourned court. Immediately after the justice's arrival there came three raps from the floor above, and O'Leary swung back the door, and disappeared with an assortment of drinkables on a tray.

The conference lasted until noon. Then the men separated outside the barroom. From the expression on the face of each one as he emerged from the door it was evident that the meeting had not produced any very cheering or conclusive results. McGaw had that vindictive, ugly, bulldog look about the eyes and mouth which always made his wife tremble when he came home. The result of the present struggle over the contract was a matter of life or death to him. His notes, secured by the chattel mortgage on his live stock, would be due in a few days. Crane had already notified him that they must be paid, and he knew enough of his money-lender, and of the anger which he had roused, to know that no extension would be granted him. Losing this contract, he had lost his only hope of paying them. Had it been awarded him, he could have found a dozen men who would have loaned him the money to take up these notes and so to pay Crane. He had comforted himself the night before with the thought that Justice Rowan could find some way to help him out of his dilemma ; that the board would vote as the justice advised, and then, of course, Tom's bid would be invalidated. Now even this hope had failed him. "Who ever heard of a woman's doing a job for a city ?" he kept repeating mechanically to himself.

Tom knew of none of these conspiracies. Had she done so they would not have caused her a moment's anxiety. Here was a fight in which no one would suffer except the head that got in her way, and she determined to hit that with all her might the moment it rose into view. This was no brewery contract, she argued with Pop, where five hundred men might be thrown out of employment, with all the attendant suffering to women and children. The village was a power nobody could boycott. Moreover, the law protected her in her rights under the award. She would therefore quietly wait until the day for signing the papers arrived, furnish her bond, and begin a work she could superintend herself. In the mean time she would continue her preparations. One thing she was resolved upon, — she would have nothing to do with the Union. Carl could lay his hand on a dozen of his countrymen who would be glad to get employment with her. If they were all like him she need have no fear in any emergency.

She bought two horses — great, strong ones — at the trolley sale, and ordered two new carts from a manufacturer in Newark, to be sent to her on the first of the coming month.

Her friends took her good fortune less calmly. Their genuine satisfaction expressed itself in a

variety of ways. Crane sent her this characteristic telegram : —

" Bully for you ! "

Babcock came all the way down to her home
to offer her his congratulations, and to tender her
what assistance she needed in tools or money.

The Union, in their deliberations, insisted that
it was the " raised bid " which had ruined the
business with McGaw and for them. It was
therefore McGaw's duty to spare no effort to
prevent her signing the contract. They had
stuck by him in times gone by ; he must now
stick by them. One point was positively insisted upon : Union men must be employed on
the work, whoever got it.

McGaw, however, was desperate. He de-
nounced Tom in a vocabulary peculiar to
himself and full of innuendoes and oaths, but
without offering any suggestion as to how his
threats against her might be carried out.

With his usual slyness, Quigg said very little
openly. He had not yet despaired of winning
Jennie's favor, and until that hope was abandoned he could hardly make up his mind which
side of the fence he was on. Crimmins was
even more indifferent in regard to the outcome;
his pay as walking delegate went on, which-
ever side won, — he could wait.

In this emergency McGaw again sought
Crimmins's assistance. He urged the importance of his getting the contract, and he promised to make Crimmins foreman on the street,
and to give him a share in the profits, if he
would help him in some way to get the work
now. The first step, he argued, was the necessity of crushing Tom. Everything else would
be easy after that. Such a task, he felt, would
not be altogether uncongenial to Crimmins, still
smarting under Tom's contemptuous treatment
of him the day he called upon her in his capacity of walking delegate.

McGaw's tempting promise made a deep impression upon Crimmins. He determined then
and there to inflict some blow on Tom Grogan
from which she could never recover. He was
equally determined on one other thing, — not to
be caught.

Early the next morning Crimmins stationed
himself outside O'Leary's, where he could get
an uninterrupted view of two streets. He stood
hunched up against the jamb of O'Leary's door
in the attitude of a corner loafer, with three parts
of his body touching the wood — hip, shoulder,
and cheek. For some time no one appeared in
sight either useful or inimical to his plans, until
Mr. James Finnegan, who was filling the morn-

ing air with one of his characteristic songs, brightened the horizon up the street to his left.

Cully's unexpected appearance at that moment produced so uncomfortable an effect upon Mr. Crimmins that that gentleman fell instantly back through the barroom door.

The boy's quick eye caught the movement, and it also caught, a moment later, Mr. Crimmins's nose and watery eye peering out again when their owner had assured himself that his escape had been unseen. Cully slackened his pace to see what new move Crimmins would make — but without the slightest sign of recognition on his face — and again broke into song. He was on his way to get the mail, and had passed McGaw's house but a few moments before, in the hope that that worthy Knight might be either leaning over the fence or seated on the broken-down porch. He was anxious McGaw should hear a few improvised stanzas of a new ballad he had composed to that delightful old negro melody, "Massa's in de cold, cold ground," in which the much-beloved Southern planter and the thoroughly hated McGaw changed places in the cemetery.

That valiant Knight was still in bed, exhausted by the labors of the previous evening. Young Billy, however, was about the stables, and so Mr. James Finnegan took occasion to tarry long enough in the road for the eldest son of his enemy to get the stanza by heart, in the hope that he might retail it to his father when he appeared.

Billy dropped his manure fork as soon as Cully had moved on again, and dodging behind the fence, followed him toward the post-office, hoping to hit the singer with a stone.

When the slinking body of McGaw's eldest son became visible to Mr. Crimmins, his face broke into creases so nearly imitative of a smile that his best friend would not have known him. He slapped the patched knees of his overalls gayly, bent over in a subdued chuckle, and disported himself in a merry and much satisfied way. His rum and watery eyes gleamed with delight, and even his chin whisker took on a new vibration. Next he laid one finger along his nose, looked about him cautiously, and said to himself in an undertone, —

"The very boy! It 'll fix McGaw dead to rights, an' ther' won't be no squealin' after it' s done."

Here he peered around the edge of one of O'Leary's drawn window-shades, and waited until Cully had passed the barroom, secured his mail, and started for home, his uninterrupted song filling the air. Then he opened the blind very cautiously, and beckoned to Billy.

Cully's eye caught the new movement as he turned the corner. His song ceased. When Mr. Finnegan had anything very serious on his mind he never sang.

When, some time after, Billy emerged from O'Leary's door, he had a two-dollar bill tightly squeezed in his right hand. Part of this he spent on his way home for a box of cigarettes; the balance he invested in a mysterious-looking tin can. The can was narrow and long, and had a screw nozzle at one end. This can Cully saw him hide in a corner of his father's stable.

XII

CULLY'S NIGHT OUT

EVER since the night Cully, with the news of the hair-breadth escape of the bid, had dashed back to Tom, waiting around the corner, he had been the hero of the hour. As she listened to his description of McGaw when her bid dropped on the table, " Lookin' like he 'd eat sumpin he could n't swaller — see ? " her face was radiant, and her sides shook with laughter. She had counted upon McGaw falling into her trap, and she was delighted over the success of her experiment. Tom had once before caught him raising a bid when he discovered that but one had been offered.

In recognition of these valuable services Tom had given Cully two tickets for a circus which was then charming the inhabitants of New Brighton, a mile or more away, and he and Carl were going the following night. Mr. Finnegan was to wear a black sack-coat, a derby hat, and a white shirt which Jennie, in the goodness of her heart, had ironed for him herself.

128

She had also ironed a scarf of Carl's, and had
laid it on the window-sill of the outer kitchen,
where Cully might find it as he passed by.

The walks home from church were now about
the only chance the lovers had of being together.
Almost every day Carl was off with the teams.
When he did come home in working hours he
would take his dinner with the men and boys
in the outer kitchen. Jennie sometimes waited
on them, but he rarely spoke to her as she
passed in and out, except with his eyes.

When Cully handed him the scarf, Carl had
already dressed himself in his best clothes, producing so marked a change in the outward appearance of the young Swede that Cully in his
admiration pronounced him "out o' sight."

Cully's metamorphosis was even more complete than Carl's. Now that the warm spring
days were approaching, Mr. Finnegan had decided that his superabundant locks were unsea-
sonable, and had therefore had his hair cropped
close to his scalp, showing here and there a
white scar, the record of some former scrim-
mage. Reaching to the edge of each ear was a
collar as stiff as pasteboard. His derby was tilted
over his left eyebrow, shading a face brimming
over with fun and expectancy. Below this was
a vermilion-colored necktie and a black coat

and trousers. His shoes sported three coats of blacking, which only partly concealed the dust-marks of his profession.

"Hully gee, Carl! but de circus's a-goin' ter be a dandy," he called out in delight, as he patted a double shuffle with his feet. "I see de picters on de fence when I come from de ferry. Dere's a chariot race out o' sight, an' a' elephant what stands on 'is head. Hold on till I see ef de Big Gray's got enough beddin' under him. He wuz awful stiff dis mornin' when I helped him up." Cully never went to bed without seeing the Gray first made comfortable for the night.

The two young fellows saw all the sights, and after filling their pockets with peanuts and themselves with pink lemonade, took their seats at last under the canvas roof, where they waited impatiently for the performance to begin.

The only departure from the ordinary routine was Cully's instant acceptance of the clown's challenge to ride the trick mule, and his winning the wager amid the plaudits of the audience, after a rough and tumble scramble in the sawdust, sticking so tight to the mule's back that a bystander remarked that the only way to get the boy off would be to "peel the mule."

When they returned it was nearly midnight.

Cully had taken off his "choker," as he called it, and had curled it outside his hat. They had walked over from the show, and the tight clutch of the collar greatly interfered with Cully's discussion of the wonderful things he had seen. Besides, the mule had ruined it completely for a second use.

It was a warm night for early spring, and Carl had his coat over his arm. When they reached the outer stable fence — the one nearest the village — Cully's keen nose scented a peculiar odor. "Who's been a-breakin' de lamp round here, Carl?" he asked, sniffing close to the ground. "Holy smoke! Look at de light in de stable — sumpin mus' be de matter wid de Big Gray, or de ole woman would n't be out dis time o' night wid a lamp. What would she be a-doin' out here, anyway?" he exclaimed in a sudden, anxious tone. "Dis ain't de road from de house. Hully gee! Look out for yer coat! De rails is a-soakin' wid ker'sene!"

At this moment a little flame shot out of the window over the Big Gray's head and licked its way up the siding, followed by a column of smoke which burst through the door in the hay loft above the stalls of the three horses next the bedroom of Carl and Cully. A window was hastily opened in Tom's house and a frightened shriek broke the stillness of the night. It was Jennie's voice, and it had a tone of something besides alarm.

What the sight of the fire had paralyzed in Carl, the voice awoke.

" No, no ! I here — I safe, Jan ! " he cried, clearing the fence with a bound.

Cully did not hear Jennie. He saw only the curling flames over the Big Gray's head. As he dashed down the slope he kept muttering the old horse's pet names, catching his breath, and calling to Carl, " Save de Gray — save Ole Blowhard ! "

Cully reached the stable first, smashed the padlock with a shovel, and rushed into the Gray's stall. Carl seized a horse bucket, and began sousing the window-sills of the harness-room, where the fire was hottest.

By this time the whole house was aroused. Tom, dazed by the sudden awakening, with her ulster thrown about her shoulders, stood barefooted on the porch. Jennie was still at the window, sobbing as if her heart would break, now that Carl was safe. Patsy had crawled out of his low crib by his mother's bed, and was stumbling downstairs, one foot at a time. Twice had Cully tried to drag the old horse clear of his stall, and twice had he fallen back for fresh air. Then came a smothered cry from inside the blinding smoke, a burst of flame lighting up the stable, and the Big Gray was pushed out, his head wrapped in Carl's coat, the Swede pressing behind, Cully coaxing him on, his arms around the horse's neck.

Hardly had the Big Gray cleared the stable when the roof of the small extension fell, and a great burst of flame shot up into the night air. All hope of rescuing the other two horses was now gone.

Tom did not stand long dazed and bewildered. In a twinkling she had drawn on a pair of men's boots over her bare feet, buckled her ulster over her nightdress, and rushed back upstairs to drag the blankets from the beds. Laden with these she sprang down the steps, called to Jennie to follow, soaked the bedding in the water-trough, and picking up the dripping mass, carried it to Carl and Cully, who, now that the Gray was safely tied to the kitchen porch, were on the roof of the tool-house, fighting the sparks that fell upon the shingles.

By this time the neighbors began to arrive from the tenements. Tom took charge of every man as soon as he got his breath, stationed two at the pump-handle, and formed a line of bucket-passers from the water-trough to Carl and Cully, who were spreading the blankets on the roof. The heat now was terrific; Carl had to shield his face with his sleeve as he threw the water. Cully lay flat on the shingles, holding to the steaming·blankets, and directing Carl's buckets with his outstretched finger when some greater spark lodged and gained headway. If they could keep these burning brands under until the heat had spent itself, they could perhaps save the tool-house and the larger stable.

All this time Patsy had stood on the porch, where Tom had left him hanging over the railing, wrapped in Jennie's shawl. He was not to move until she came for him : she wanted him out of the way of trampling feet. Now and then she would turn anxiously, catch sight of his wizened face dazed with fright, wave her hand to him encouragingly, and work on.

Suddenly the little fellow gave a cry of terror and slid from the porch, trailing the shawl after him, his crutch jerking over the ground, his sobs almost choking him.

"Mammy! Cully! Stumpy's tied in the loft! Oh, somebody help me! He's in the loft! Oh, please, please!"

In the roar of the flames nobody heard him. The noise of axes beating down the burning fences drowned all other sounds. At this moment Tom was standing on a cart, passing up the buckets to Carl. Cully had crawled to the ridgepole of the tool-house to watch both sides of the threatened roof.

The little cripple made his way slowly into the crowd nearest the sheltered side of the tool-house, pulling at the men's coats, pleading with them to save his goat, his Stumpy.

On this side was a door opening into a room where the chains were kept. From it rose a short flight of six or seven steps leading to the loft. This loft had two big doors — one closed, nearest the fire, and the other wide open, fronting the house. When the roof of the burning stable fell, the wisps of straw in the cracks of the closed door burst into flame.

Within three feet of this blazing mass, shivering with fear, tugging at his rope, his eyes bursting from his head, stood Stumpy, his piteous bleatings unheard in the surrounding roar. A child's head appeared above the floor, followed by a cry of joy as the boy flung himself upon the straining rope. The next instant a half-frenzied goat sprang through the open door and landed in the yard below, in the midst of the startled men and women.

Tom was on the cart when she saw this streak

135

of light flash out of the darkness of the loft door and disappear. Her eyes instinctively turned to look at Patsy in his place on the porch. Then a cry of horror burst from the crowd, silenced instantly as a piercing shriek filled the air.

"My God! It's me Patsy!"

Bareheaded in the open doorway of the now blazing loft, a silhouette against the flame, his little white gown reaching to his knees, his crutch gone, the stifling smoke rolling out in great whirls above his head, stood the cripple!

Tom hurled herself into the crowd, knocking the men out of her way, and ran towards the chain-room door. At this instant a man in his shirt-sleeves dropped from the smoking roof, sprang in front of her, and caught her in his arms.

"No, not you go; Carl go!" he said in a firm voice, holding her fast.

Before she could speak he snatched a handkerchief from a woman's neck, plunged it into the water of the horse-trough, bound it about his head, dashed up the short flight of steps, and crawled toward the terror-stricken child. There was a quick clutch, a bound back, and the smoke rolled over them, shutting man and child from view.

The crowd held its breath as it waited. A

man with his hair singed and his shirt on fire
staggered from the side door. In his arms he
carried the almost lifeless boy, his face covered
by the handkerchief.

A woman rushed up, caught the boy in her
arms, and sank on her knees. The man reeled
and fell.

When Carl regained consciousness, Jennie was
bending over him, chafing his hands and bath-
ing his face. Patsy was on the sofa, wrapped
in Jennie's shawl. Pop was fanning him. Carl's
wet handkerchief, the old man said, had kept
the boy from suffocating.

The crowd had begun to disperse. The
neighbors and strangers had gone their several
ways. The tenement-house mob were on the
road to their beds. Many friends had stopped
to sympathize, and even the bitterest of Tom's
enemies said they were glad it was no worse.

When the last of them had left the yard,
Tom, tired out with anxiety and hard work,
threw herself down on the porch. The morning was already breaking, the gray streaks of
dawn brightening the east. From her seat she
could hear through the open door the soothing
tones of Jennie's voice as she talked to her
lover, and the hoarse whispers of Carl in reply.

He had recovered his breath again, and was but little worse for his scorching except in his speech. Jennie was in the kitchen, making some coffee for the exhausted workers, and he was helping her.

Tom realized fully all that had happened. She knew who had saved Patsy's life. She remembered how he laid her boy in her arms, and she still saw the deathly pallor in his face as he staggered and fell. What had he not done for her and her household since he entered her service? If he loved Jennie, and she him, was it his fault? Why did she rebel, and refuse this man a place in her home? Then she thought of her own Tom no longer with her, and of her fight alone and without him. What would he have thought of it? How would he have advised her to act? He had always hoped such great things for Jennie! Would he now be willing to give her to this stranger? If she could only talk to her Tom about it all!

As she sat, her head in her hand, the smoking stable, the eager, wild-eyed crowd, the dead horses, faded away and became to her as a dream. She heard nothing but the voice of Jennie and her lover, saw only the white face of her boy. A sickening sense of utter loneliness swept over her. She rose and moved away.

During all this time Cully was watching the dying embers, and when all danger was over, — only the small stable with its two horses had been destroyed, — he led the Big Gray back to the pump, washed his head, sponging his eyes and mouth, and housed him in the big stable. Then he vanished.

Immediately on leaving the Big Gray, Cully had dodged behind the stable, run rapidly up the hill, keeping close to the fence, and had come out behind a group of scattering specta-tors. There he began a series of complicated manœuvres, mostly on his toes, lifting his head over those of the crowd, and ending in a sud-den dart forward and as sudden a halt, within a few inches of young Billy McGaw's coat-collar.

Billy turned pale, but held his ground. He felt sure Cully would not dare attack him with so many others about. Then, again, the glow of the smouldering cinders had a fascination for him that held him to the spot.

Cully also seemed spellbound. The only view of the smoking ruins that satisfied him seemed to be the one he caught over young McGaw's shoulder. He moved closer and closer, sniffing about cautiously, as a dog would on a trail. Indeed, the closer he got to Billy's coat the

139

more absorbed he seemed to be in the view beyond.

Here an extraordinary thing happened. There
was a dipping of Cully's head between Billy's
legs, a raising of both arms, grabbing Billy
around the waist, and in a flash the hope of
the house of McGaw was swept off his feet,
Cully beneath him, and in full run toward Tom's
house. The bystanders laughed; they thought
it only a boyish trick. Billy kicked and struggled, but Cully held on. When they were clear
of the crowd, Cully shook him to the ground
and grabbed him by the coat-collar.

"Say, young feller, where wuz ye when de
fire started?"

At this Billy broke into a howl, and one of the
crowd, some distance off, looked up. Cully
clapped his hand over the boy's mouth. "None
o' that, or I'll mash yer mug — see?" standing over him with clenched fist.

"I warn't nowheres," stammered Billy.
"Say, take yer hands off 'n me — ye ain't" —

"T' 'ell I ain't! Ye answer me straight —
see? — or I'll punch yer face in," tightening
his grasp. "What wuz ye a-doin' when de
circus come out — an', anoder t'ing, what's
dis cologne yer got on yer coat? Maybe next
time ye climb a fence ye'll keep from spillin'

140

it, see? Oh, I'm onter ye. Ye set de stable afire. Dat's what's de matter."

" I hope I may die — I wuz a-carryin' de can er ker'sene home, an' when de roof fell in I wuz up on de fence so I c'u'd see de fire, an' de can slipped " —

" What fence? " demanded Cully, shaking him as a terrier would a rat.

" Why, dat fence on de hill."

That was enough for Cully. He had his man. The lie had betrayed him. Without a word he jerked the cowardly boy from the ground, and marched him straight into the kitchen.

" Say, Carl, I got de firebug. Ye kin smell der ker'sene on his clo'es."

XIII

MR. QUIGG DRAWS A PLAN

McGAW had watched the fire from his upper window with mingled joy and fear — joy that Tom's property was on fire, and fear that it would be put out before she would be ruined. He had been waiting all the evening for Crimmins, who had failed to arrive. Billy had not been at home since supper, so he could get no details as to the amount of the damage from that source. In this emergency he sent next morning for Quigg to make a reconnaissance in the vicinity of the enemy's camp, ascertain how badly Tom had been crippled, and learn whether her loss would prevent her signing the contract the following night. Mr. Quigg accepted the mission, the more willingly because he wanted to settle certain affairs of his own. Jennie had avoided him lately, — why he could not tell, — and he determined, before communicating to his employer the results of his inquiries about Tom, to know exactly what his own chances were with the girl. He could slip

over to the house while Tom was in the city,
and leave before she returned.

On his way, the next day, he robbed a garden fence of a mass of lilacs, breaking off the
leaves as he walked. When he reached the
door of the big stable he stopped for a moment,
glanced cautiously in to see if he could find any
preparations for the new work, and then, making a mental note of the surroundings, followed
the path to the porch.

Pop opened the door. He knew Quigg only
by sight, — an unpleasant sight, he thought, as
he looked into his hesitating, wavering eyes.

"It's a bad fire ye had, Mr. Mullins," said
Quigg, seating himself in the rocker, the blossoms half strangled in his grasp.

"Yis, purty bad, but small loss, thank God,"
remarked Pop quietly.

"That lets her out of the contract, don't
it?" inquired Quigg. "She'll be short of
horses now."

Pop made no answer. He did not intend to
give Mr. Quigg any information that might
comfort him.

"Were ye insured?" asked Quigg in a cau-
tious tone, his eyes on the lilacs.

"Oh, yis, ivery pinny on what was burned,
so Mary tells me."

143

Quigg caught his breath; the rumor in the village was the other way. Why did n't Crimmins make a clean sweep of it and burn 'em all at once? he said to himself.

"I brought some flowers over for Miss Jennie," said Quigg, regaining his composure. "Is she in?"

"Yis; I 'll call her." Gentle and apparently harmless as Gran'pop was, men like Quigg somehow never looked him steadily in the eye.

"I was tellin' Mr. Mullins I brought ye over some flowers," said Quigg, turning to Jennie as she entered, and handing her the bunch without leaving his seat, as if it had been a pair of shoes.

"You 're very kind, Mr. Quigg," said the girl, laying them on the table, and still standing.

"I hear'd your brother Patsy was near smothered till Dutchy got him out. Was ye there?"

Jennie bit her lip and her heart quickened. Carl's sobriquet in the village, coming from such lips, sent the hot blood to her cheeks.

"Yes, Mr. Nilsson saved his life," she answered slowly, with girlish dignity, a backward rush filling her heart as she remembered Carl

staggering out of the burning stable, Patsy held
close to his breast.

"The fellers in Rockville say ye think it was
set afire. I see Justice Rowan turned Billy Mc-
Gaw loose. Do ye suspect anybody else ? Some
says a tramp crawled in and upset his pipe."

This lie was coined on the spot and issued
immediately to see if it would pass.

"Mother says she knows who did it, and
it 'll all come out in time. Cully found the can
this morning," Jennie replied, leaning against
the table.

Quigg's jaw fell and his brow knit as Jennie
spoke. That was just like the fool, he said to
himself. Why did n't he get the stuff in a bottle and then break it ?

But the subject was too dangerous to linger
over, so he began talking of the dance down at
the Town Hall, and the meeting last Sunday
after church. He asked her if she would go with
him to the "sociable" they were going to have
at No. 4 Truck-house ; and when she said she
could n't, — that her mother did n't want her
to go out, etc., — Quigg moved his chair closer,
with the remark that the old woman was always
putting her oar in and spoiling things ; the
way she was going on with the Union would
ruin her ; she 'd better join in with the boys,

and be friendly; they 'd " down her yet if she did n't."

" I hope nothing will happen to mother, Mr. Quigg," said Jennie in an anxious tone, as she sank into a chair.

Quigg misunderstood the movement, and moved his own closer.

" There won't nothin' happen any more, Jennie, if you 'll do as I say."

It was the first time he had ever called her by her first name. She could not understand how he dared. She wished Carl would come in.

" Will you do it ?" asked Quigg eagerly, his cunning face and mean eyes turned toward her.

Jennie never raised her head. Her cheeks were burning. Quigg went on, —

" I 've been keepin' company with ye, Jennie, all winter, and the fellers is guyin' me about it. You know I 'm solid with the Union and can help yer mother, and if ye 'll let me speak to Father McCluskey next Sunday " —

The girl sprang from her chair.

" I won't have you talk that way to me, Dennis Quigg ! I never said a word to you, and you know it." Her mother's spirit was now flashing in her eyes. "You ought to be ashamed of yourself to come here — and " —

Then she broke down.

Another woman would have managed it differently, perhaps, — by a laugh, a smile of contempt, or a frigid refusal. This mere child, stung to the quick by Quigg's insult, had only her tears in defence. The Walking Delegate turned his head and looked out of the window. Then he caught up his hat and without a word to the sobbing girl hastily left the room.

Tom was just entering the lower gate. Quigg saw her and tried to dodge behind the tool-house, but it was too late, so he faced her. Tom's keen eye caught the sly movement and the quickly altered expression. Some new trickery was in the air, she knew; she detected it in every line of Quigg's face. What was McGaw up to now? she asked herself. Was he after Carl and the men, or getting ready to burn the other stable?

"Good-morning, Mr. Quigg. Ain't ye lost?" she asked coldly.

"Oh, no," said Quigg, with a forced laugh. "I come over to see if I could help about the fire."

It was the first thing that came into his head; he had hoped to pass with only a nod of greeting.

"Did ye?" replied Tom thoughtfully. She saw he had lied, but she led him on. "What

147

kind of help did ye think of givin' ? The insurance company will pay the money, the two
horses is buried, an' we begin diggin' post-holes
for a new stable in the mornin'. Perhaps ye
were thinkin' of lendin' a hand yerself. If ye
did, I can put ye alongside of Carl ; one shovel
might do for both of ye."

Quigg colored and laughed uneasily. Somebody had told her, then, how Carl had threatened him with uplifted shovel when he tried to
coax the Swede away.

" No, I 'm not diggin' these days ; but I 've
got a pull wid the insurance adjuster, and might
git an extra allowance for yer." This was cut
from whole cloth. He had never known an adjuster in his life.

" What 's that ? " asked Tom, still looking
square at him, Quigg squirming under her
glance like a worm on a pin.

" Well, the company can't tell how much
feed was in the bins, and tools, and sech like,"
he said, with another laugh.

A laugh is always a safe parry when a pair
of clear gray searchlight eyes are cutting into
one like a rapier.

" An' yer idea is for me to git paid for stuff
that was n't burned up, is it ? "

" Well, that 's as how the adjuster says.

Sometimes he sees it an' sometimes he don't,
—that 's where the pull comes in."

Tom put her arms akimbo, her favorite attitude when her anger began to rise.

"Oh, I see! The pull is in bribin' the adjuster, as ye call him, so he can cheat the
company."

Quigg shrugged his shoulders; that part of
the transaction was a mere trifle. What were
companies made for but to be cheated?

Tom stood for a minute looking him all over.

"Dennis Quigg," she said slowly, weighing
each word, her eyes riveted on his face, "ye 're
a very sharp young man; ye 're so very sharp
that I wonder ye 've gone so long without cut-
tin' yerself. But one thing I tell ye, an' that
is, if ye keep on the way ye 're a-goin' ye 'll
land where you belong, and that 's up the river
in a potato-bug suit of clothes. Turn yer head
this way, Quigg. Did ye niver in yer whole
life think there was somethin' worth the havin'
in bein' honest an' clean an' square, an' holdin'
yer head up like a man, instead of skulkin'
round like a thief? What ye 're up to this
mornin' I don't know yet, but I want to tell ye
it 's the wrong time o' day for ye to make calls,
and the night 's not much better, unless ye 're
particularly invited."

Quigg smothered a curse and turned on his heel toward the village. When he reached O'Leary's, Dempsey of the executive committee met him at the door. He and McGaw had spent the whole morning in devising plans to keep Tom out of the board-room.

Quigg's report was not reassuring. She would be paid her insurance money, he said, and would certainly be at the meeting that night.

The three adjourned to the room over the bar. McGaw began pacing the floor, his long arms hooked behind his back. He had passed a sleepless night, and every hour now added to his anxiety. His face was a dull gray yellow, and his eyes were sunken. Now and then he would tug at his collar nervously. As he walked he clutched his fingers, burying the nails in the palms, the red hair on his wrists bristling like spiders' legs. Dempsey sat at the table watching him calmly out of the corner of his eye.

After a pause Quigg leaned over, his lips close to Dempsey's ear. Then he drew a plan on the back of an old wine-list. It marked the position of the door in Tom's stable, and that of a path which ran across lots and was concealed from her house by a low fence. Dempsey studied it a moment, nodding at Quigg's whispered explanations, and passed it to Mc-

150

Gaw, repeating Quigg's words. McGaw stopped
and bent his head. A dull gleam flashed out of
his smouldering eyes. The lines of his face
hardened and his jaw tightened. For some minutes he stood irresolute, gazing vacantly over
the budding trees through the window. Then
he turned sharply, swallowed a brimming glass
of raw whiskey, and left the room.

When the sound of his footsteps had died
away, Dempsey looked at Quigg meaningly and
gave a low laugh.

XIV

BLOSSOM WEEK

IT was "blossom week," and every garden
and hedge flaunted its bloom in the soft air.
All about was the perfume of flowers, the odor
of fresh grass, and that peculiar earthy smell
of new-made garden beds but lately sprinkled.
Behind the hill overlooking the harbor the sun
was just sinking into the sea. Some sentinel
cedars guarding its crest stood out in clear relief against the golden light. About their tops,
in wide circles, swooped a flock of crows.

Gran'pop and Tom sat on the front porch,
their chairs touching, his hand on hers. She
had been telling him of Quigg's visit that morning. She had changed her dress for a new one.
The dress was of brown cloth, and had been
made in the village, — tight where it should be
loose, and loose where it should be tight. She
had put it on, she told Pop, to make a credit-
able appearance before the board that night.

Jennie was flitting in and out between the
sitting-room and the garden, her hands full of

blossoms, filling the china jars on the mantel.
None of them contained Quigg's contribution.
Patsy was flat on his back on the small patch
of green surrounding the porch, playing circus-
elephant with Stumpy, who stood over him with
levelled head.

Up the hill, but a few rods away, Cully was
grazing the Big Gray, the old horse munching
tufts of fresh, sweet grass sprinkled with dandelions. Cully walked beside him. Now and then
he lifted one of his legs, examining the hoof
critically for possible tender places.

There was nothing the matter with the Gray :
the old horse was still sound ; but it satisfied
Cully to be assured, and it satisfied, too, a certain yearning tenderness in his heart toward his
old chum. Once in a while he would pat the
Gray's neck, smoothing his ragged, half-worn
mane, addressing him all the while in words
of endearment expressed in a slang positively
profane and utterly without meaning except to
these two.

Suddenly Jennie's cheek flushed as she came
out on the porch. Carl was coming up the path.
The young Swede was bareheaded, the short
blond curls glistening in the light; his throat
was bare too, so that one could see the big mus-
cles in his neck. Jennie always liked him with

his throat bare ; it reminded her of a hero she had once seen in a play, who stormed a fort and rescued all the starving women.

"Da brown horse seek ; batta come to stabble an' see him," Carl said, going direct to the porch, where he stood in front of Tom, resting one hand on his hip, his eyes never wandering from her face. He knew where Jennie was, but he never looked.

"What's the matter with him?" asked Tom, her thoughts far away at the moment.

"I don' know ; he no eat da oats en da box."

"Will he drink?" inquired Tom, awakening to the importance of the information.

"Yas ; 'mos' two buckets."

"It's fever he's got," she said, turning to Pop. "I thought that yisterday noon when I seen him a-workin'. All right, Carl ; I'll be down before I go to the board meetin'. An' see here, Carl ; ye'd better git ready to go wid me. I'll start in a couple o' hours. Will it suit ye, Gran'pop, if Carl goes wid me?" — patting her father's shoulder. "If ye keep on a-worritin' I'll hev to hire a cop to follow me round."

Carl lingered for a moment on the steps. Perhaps Tom had some further orders ; perhaps, too, Jennie would come out again. Involunta-

154

rily his eye wandered toward the open door, and then he turned to go. Jennie's heart sprang up in her throat. She had seen from behind the curtains the shade of disappointment that crossed her lover's face. She could suffer herself, but she could not see Carl unhappy. In an instant she was beside her mother. Anything to keep Carl, she did not care what.

"Oh, Carl, will you bring the ladder so I can reach the long branches?" she said, her quick wit helping her with a subterfuge.

Carl turned and glanced at Tom. He felt the look in her face and could read her thoughts.

If Tom had heard Jennie she never moved. This affair must end in some way, she said to herself. Why had she not sent him away long before? How could she do it now when he had risked his life to save Patsy?

Then she answered firmly, still without turning her head, "No, Jennie; there won't be time. Carl must get ready to" —

Pop laid his hand on hers.

"There's plinty o' toime, Mary. Ye'll git the ladder behint the kitchen door, Carl. I hed it ther' mesilf this mornin'."

Carl found the ladder, steadied it against the tree, and guided Jennie's little feet till they reached the topmost round, holding on to her

skirts so that she should not fall. Above their
heads the branches twined and interlaced, shed-
ding their sweetest blossoms over their happy
upturned faces. The old man's eyes lightened
as he watched them for some moments; then,
turning to Tom, his voice full of tenderness,
he said, —

"Carl's a foine lad, Mary; ye'll do no better for Jinnie."

Tom did not answer; her eyes were on the
cedars where the crows were flying, black sil-
houettes against the yellow sky.

"Did I shtop ye an' break yer heart whin ye
wint off wid yer own Tom? What wuz he but
an honest lad thet loved ye, an' he wid not a
pinny in his pocket but the fare that brought
ye both to the new counthry?"

Tom's eyes filled. She could not see the
cedars now. All the hill was swimming in
light.

"Oi hev watched Carl sence he fust come,
Mary. It's a good mither some'er's as has
lost a foine b'y. W'u'd n't ye be lonely yersilf
ef ye'd come here wid nobody to touch yer
hand?"

Tom shivered and covered her face. Who
was more lonely than she — she who had hun-
gered for the same companionship that she was

denying Jennie; she who had longed for somebody to stand between her and the world, some
hand to touch, some arm to lean on; she who
must play the man always, — the man and the
mother too!

Pop went on, stroking her strong, firm hand
with his stiff, shrivelled fingers. He never
looked at her; his face too was now turned
toward the dying sun.

"Do ye remimber the day ye left me in the
ould counthry, Mary, wid yer own Tom; an'
how I walked wid ye to the turnin' of the road?
It wuz spring thin, an' the hedges all white wid
blossoms. Look at thim two over there, Mary,
wid their arms full o' flowers. Don't be breakin'
their hearts, child."

Tom turned and slipped her arm around the
old man's neck, her head sinking on his shoulder. The tears were under her eyelids; her
heart was bursting; only her pride sustained
her. Then in a half-whispered voice, like a
child telling its troubles, she said, —

"Ye don't know, ye don't know, Gran'pop.
The dear God knows it's not on account of
meself. It's Tom I'm thinkin' of night an' day,
— me Tom, me Tom. She's his child as well
as mine. If he could only help me! He wanted
such great things for Jennie. It ud be easier if

he had n't saved Patsy. Don't speak to me ag'in about it, father dear; it hurts me."

The old man rose from his chair and walked slowly into the house. All his talks with his daughter ended in this way. It was always what Tom would have thought. Why should a poor crazy cripple like her husband, shut up in an asylum, make trouble for Jennie?

When the light faded and the trees grew indistinct in the gloom, Tom still sat where Pop had left her. Soon the shadows fell in the little valley, and the hill beyond the cedars lost itself in the deepening haze that now crept in from the tranquil sea.

Carl's voice calling to Cully to take in the Gray roused her to consciousness. She pushed back her chair, stood for an instant watching Carl romping with Patsy, and then walked slowly toward the stable.

By the time she reached the water-trough her old manner had returned. Her step became once more elastic and firm; her strong will asserted itself. She had work to do, and at once. In two hours the board would meet. She needed all her energies and resources. The lovers must wait; she could not decide any question for them now.

As she passed the stable window a man in a

fur cap raised his head cautiously above the low fence and shrank back into the shadow.

Tom threw open the door and felt along the sill for the lantern and matches. They were not in their accustomed place. The man crouched, ran noiselessly toward the rear entrance, and crept in behind a stall. Tom laid her hand on the haunches of the horse and began rolling back his blanket. The man drew himself up slowly, until his shoulders were on a level with the planking. Tom moved a step and turned her face. The man raised his arm, whirled a hammer high in the air, and brought it down upon her head.

When Cully led the Big Gray into his stall, a moment later, he stepped into a pool of blood.

XV

IN THE SHADOW OF DEATH

AT the appointed hour the Board of Trustees met in the hall over the post-office. The usual loungers filled the room, — members of the Union, and others who had counted on a piece of the highway pie when it was cut. Dempsey, Crimmins, and Quigg sat outside the rail, against the wall. They were waiting for McGaw, who had not been seen since the afternoon.

The president was in his accustomed place. The five gentlemen of leisure, the veterinary surgeon, and the other trustees occupied their several chairs. The roll had been called, and every man had answered to his name. The occasion being one of much importance, a full board was required.

As the minute-hand neared the hour of nine Dempsey became uneasy. He started every time a newcomer mounted the stairs. Where was McGaw? No one had seen him since he swallowed the tumblerful of whiskey and

160

disappeared from O'Leary's, a few hours before.

The president rapped for order, and announced that the board was ready to sign the contract with Thomas Grogan for the hauling and delivery of the broken stone required for public highways.

There was no response.

"Is Mrs. Grogan here?" asked the president, looking over the room and waiting for a reply.

"Is any one here who represents her?" he repeated, after a pause, rising in his seat as he spoke.

No one answered. The only sound heard in the room was that of the heavy step of a man mounting the stairs.

"Is there any one here who can speak for Mrs. Thomas Grogan?" called the president again in a louder voice.

"I can," said the man with the heavy tread, who proved to be the foreman at the brewery. "She won't live till mornin'; one of her horses kicked her and broke her skull, so McGaw told me."

"Broke her skull! My God, man, how do you know?" demanded the president, his voice trembling with excitement.

Every man's face was now turned toward the newcomer; a momentary thrill of horror ran through the assemblage.

"I heard it at the druggist's. One of her boys was over for medicine. Dr. Mason sewed up her head. He was drivin' by, on his way to Quarantine, when it happened."

"What Dr. Mason?" asked a trustee, eager for details.

"The man what used to be at Quarantine seven years ago. He's app'inted ag'in."

Dempsey caught up his hat and hurriedly left the room, followed by Quigg and Crimmins. McGaw, he said to himself, as he ran downstairs, must be blind drunk, not to come to the meeting. "——him! What if he gives everything away!" he added aloud.

"This news is awful!" said the president. "I am very sorry for Mrs. Grogan and her children — she was a fine woman. It is a serious matter, too, for the village. The highway work ought to commence at once; the roads need it. We may now have to advertise again. That would delay everything for a month."

"Well, there's other bids," said another trustee, — one of the gentlemen of leisure, — ignoring the president's sympathy, and hopeful

162

now of a possible slice on his own account.
" What's the matter with McGaw's proposal ?
There's not much difference in the price. Per-
haps he would come down to the Grogan figure.
Is Mr. McGaw here, or anybody who can speak
for him ? "

Justice Rowan sat against the wall. The
over-zealous trustee had exactly expressed his
own wishes and anxieties. He wanted McGaw's
chances settled at once. If they failed, there
was Rowan's own brother who might come in
for the work, — the justice sharing, of course, in
the profits.

" In the absence of me client," said Rowan,
looking about the room, and drawing in his
breath with an important air, " I suppose I can
ripresint him. I think, however, that if your
honorable boord will go on with the other business before you, Mr. McGaw will be on hand
in half an hour himself. In the mean time I will
hunt him up."

" I move," said the Scotch surgeon, in a
voice that showed how deeply he had been
affected, " that the whole matter be laid on
the table for a week, until we know for certain
whether poor Mrs. Grogan is killed or not. I
can hardly credit it. It is very seldom that a
horse kicks a woman."

163

Nobody having seconded this motion, the chair did not put it. The fact was that every man was afraid to move. The majority of the trustees, who favored McGaw, were in the dark as to what effect Tom's death would have upon the bids. The law might require readvertising and hence a new competition, and perhaps somebody much worse for them than Tom might turn up and take the work, — somebody living outside of the village. Then none of them would get a finger in the pie. Worse than all, the cutting of it might have to be referred to the corporation counsel, Judge Bowker. What his opinion would be was past finding out. He was beyond the reach of "pulls," and followed the law to the letter.

The minority — a minority of two, the president and the veterinary surgeon — began to distrust the spirit of McGaw's adherents. It looked to the president as if a "deal" were in the air.

The Scotchman, practical, sober-minded, sensible man as he was, had old-fashioned ideas of honesty and fair play. He had liked Tom from the first time he saw her, — he had looked after her stables professionally, — and he did not intend to see her, dead or alive, thrown out without making a fight for her.

164

"I move," said he, "that the president appoint a committee of this board to jump into the nearest wagon, drive to Mrs. Grogan's, and find out whether she is still alive. If she's dead, that settles it; but if she's alive, I will protest against anything being done about this matter for ten days. It won't take twenty minutes to find out; meantime we can take up the unfinished business of the last meeting."

One of the gentlemen of leisure seconded this motion; it was carried unanimously, and this gentleman of leisure was himself appointed courier, and left the room in a hurry. He had hardly reached the street when he was back again, followed closely by Dempsey, Quigg, Crimmins, Justice Rowan, and, last of all, fumbling with his fur cap, deathly pale, and entirely sober — Dan McGaw.

"There's no use of my going," said the courier trustee, taking his seat. "Grogan won't live an hour, if she ain't dead now. She had a sick horse that wanted looking after, and she went into the stable without a light, and he let drive, and broke her skull. She's got a gash the length of your hand — wasn't that it, Mr. Mc-Gaw ?"

McGaw nodded his head.

"Yes; that's about it," he said. The voice

165

seemed to come from his stomach, it was so hollow.

"Did you see her, Mr. McGaw?" asked the Scotchman in a positive tone.

"How c'u'd I be a-seein' her whin I been in New Yorruk 'mos' all day? D' ye think I 'm runnin' roun' to ivery stable in the place? I wuz a-comin' 'cross lots whin I heared it. They says the horse had blin' staggers."

"How do you know, then?" asked the Scotchman suspiciously. "Who told you the horse kicked her?"

"Well, I dunno; I think it wuz some un" —
Dempsey looked at him and knit his brow. McGaw stopped.

"Don't you know enough of a horse to know he could n't kick with blind staggers?" insisted the Scotchman.

McGaw did not answer.

"Does anybody know any of the facts connected with this dreadful accident to Mrs. Grogan?" asked the president. "Have you heard anything, Mr. Quigg?"

Mr. Quigg had heard absolutely nothing, and had not seen Mrs. Grogan for months. Mr. Crimmins was equally ignorant, and so were several other gentlemen. Here a voice came from the back of the room.

"I met Dr. Mason, sir, an hour ago, after he had attended Tom Grogan. He was on his way to Quarantine in his buggy. He said he left her insensible after dressin' the wound. He thought she might not live till mornin'."

"May I ask your name, sir?" asked the president in a courteous tone.

"Peter Lathers. I am yardmaster at the U. S. Lighthouse Depot."

The title, and the calm way in which Lathers spoke, convinced the president and the room. Everybody realized that Tom's life hung by a thread. The Scotchman still had a lingering doubt. He also wished to clear up the blind-staggers theory.

"Did he say how she was hurt?" asked the Scotchman.

"Yes. He said he was a-drivin' by when they picked her up, and he was dead sure that somebody had hid in the stable and knocked her on the head with a club."

McGaw steadied himself with his hand and grasped the seat of his chair. The sweat was rolling from his face. He seemed afraid to look up, lest some other eye might catch his own and read his thoughts. If he had only seen Lathers come in!

Lathers's announcement, coupled with the

Scotchman's well-known knowledge of equine diseases, discrediting the blind-staggers theory, produced a profound sensation. Heads were put together, and low whispers were heard. Dempsey, Quigg, and Crimmins did not move a muscle.

The Scotchman again broke the silence.

"There seems to be no question, gentlemen, that the poor woman is badly hurt; but she is still alive, and while she breathes we have no right to take this work from her. It's not decent to serve a woman so; and I think, too, it's illegal. I again move that the whole matter be laid upon the table."

This motion was not put, nobody seconding it.

Then Justice Rowan rose. The speech of the justice was seasoned with a brogue as delicate in flavor as the garlic in a Spanish salad.

"Mr. President and Gintlemen of the Honorable Boord of Village Trustees," said the justice, throwing back his coat. The elaborate opening compelled attention at once. Such courtesies were too seldom heard in their deliberations, thought the members, as they lay back in their chairs to listen. "No wan can be moore pained than meself that so estimable a woman as Mrs. Grogan — a woman who fills so

168

honorably her every station in life — should at this moment be stricken down either by the hand of an assassin or the hoof of a horse. Such acts in a law-abidin' community like Rockville bring with them the deepest detistation and the profoundest sympathy. No wan, I am sure, is more touched by her misforchune than me worthy friend Mr. Daniel McGaw, who by this direct interposition of Providence is foorced into the position of being compelled to assert his rights befoore your honorable body, with full assurance that there is no tribunal in the land to which he could apply which would lind a more willing ear."

It was this sort of thing that made Rowan popular.

"But, gintlemen," — here the justice curry-combed his front hair with his fingers, greasy, jet-black hair, worn long, as befitted his position, — "this is not a question of sympathy, but a question of law. Your honorable boord advertoised some time since for certain supplies needed for the growth and development of this most important of the villages of Staten Island. In this call it was most positively and clearly stated that the contract was to be awarded to the lowest responsible bidder who gave the proper bonds. Two risponses were made to this

call, wan by Mrs. Grogan, acting on behalf of
her husband, — well known to be a hopeless
cripple in wan of the many charitable institoo-
tions of our noble State, — and the other by our
distinguished fellow townsman, Mr. Daniel Mc-
Gaw, whom I have the honor to ripresint. With
that strict sinse of justice which has always
characterized the decisions of this honorable
boord, the contract was promptly awarded to
Thomas Grogan, he being the lowest bidder ;
and my client, Daniel McGaw, — honest Daniel McGaw I should call him if his presence did
not deter me, — stood wan side in obadience to
the will of the people and the laws of the State,
and accepted his defate with that calmness
which always distinguishes the hard-workin'
sons of toil, who are not only the bone and
sinoo of our land, but its honor and proide. But,
gintlemen," — running his hand lightly through
his hair, and then laying it in the bulging lapels
of his now half-buttoned coat, — "there were
other conditions accompanying these proposals ;
to wit, that within tin days from said openin'
the successful bidder should appear befoore this
honorable body, and then and there duly afix
his signatoor to the aforesaid contracts, already
prepared by the attorney of this boord, my
honored associate, Judge Bowker. Now, gin-

tlemen, I ask you to look at the clock, whose calm face, like a rising moon, presides over the deliberations of this boord, and note the passin' hour ; and then I ask you to cast your eyes over this vast assemblage and see if Thomas Grogan, or any wan ripresinting him or her, or who in any way is connected with him or her, is within the confines of this noble hall, to execute the mandates of this distinguished boord. Can it be believed for an instant that if Mrs. Grogan, acting for her partly dismimbered husband, Mr. Thomas Grogan, had intinded to sign this contract, she would not have dispatched on the wings of the wind some Mecury, fleet of foot, to infarm this boord of her desire for postponement ? I demand in the interests of justice that the contract be awarded to the lowest risponsible bidder who is ready to sign the contract with proper bonds, whether that bidder is Grogan, McGaw, Jones, Robinson, or Smith.''

There was a burst of applause and great stamping of feet ; the tide of sympathy had changed. Rowan had perhaps won a few more votes. This pleased him, evidently, more than his hope of cutting the contract pie. McGaw began to regain some of his color and lose some of his nervousness. Rowan's speech had quieted him.

The president gravely rapped for order. It was wonderful how much backbone and dignity and self-respect the justice's very flattering remarks had injected into the nine trustees — no, eight, for the Scotchman fully understood and despised Rowan's oratorical powers.

The Scotchman was on his feet in an instant.

"I have listened," he said, "to the talk that Justice Rowan has given us. It 's very fine and tonguey, but it smothers up the facts. You can't rob this woman " —

" Question! question! " came from half a dozen throats.

"What 's your pleasure, gentlemen ?" asked the president, pounding with his gavel.

"I move," said the courier member, "that the contract be awarded to Mr. Daniel McGaw as the lowest bidder, provided he can sign the contract to-night with proper bonds."

Four members seconded it.

"Is Mr. McGaw's bondsman present?" asked the president, rising.

Justice Rowan rose, and bowed with the air of a foreign banker accepting a government loan.

"I have that honor, Mr. Prisident. I am willing to back Mr. McGaw to the extent of me humble possissions, which are ample, I trust,

172

SHE STEADIED HERSELF FOR A MOMENT AND TOOK A ROLL
OF PAPERS FROM HER DRESS.

for the purposes of this contract," — looking
around with an air of entire confidence.

"Gentlemen, are you ready for the question ? " asked the president.

At this instant there was a slight commotion
at the end of the hall. Half a dozen men nearest the door left their seats and crowded to the
top of the staircase. Then came a voice outside, " Fall back ! Don't block up the door !
Get back there ! " The excitement was so great
that the proceedings of the board were stopped.
The throng parted. The men near the table
stood still. An ominous silence suddenly pre-
vailed. Daniel McGaw twisted his head, turned
ghastly white, and would have fallen from his
chair but for Dempsey.

Advancing through the door with slow, measured tread, her long cloak reaching to her feet ;
erect, calm, fearless ; her face like chalk ; her
lips compressed, stifling the agony of every
step ; her eyes deep-sunken, black-rimmed,
burning like coals ; her brow bound with a
blood-stained handkerchief that barely hid the
bandages beneath, — came Tom.

The deathly hush was unbroken. The men
fell back with white, scared faces to let her
pass. McGaw cowered in his chair. Dempsey's eyes glistened, a half sigh of relief escap-

ing him. Crimmins had not moved; the apparition stunned him.

On she came, her eyes fixed on the president, till she reached the table. Then she steadied herself for a moment, took a roll of papers from her dress, and sank into a chair.

No one spoke. The crowd pressed closer. Those outside the rail noiselessly mounted the benches and chairs, craning their necks. Every eye was fixed upon her.

Slowly and carefully she unrolled the contract, spreading it out before her, picked up a pen from the table, and without a word wrote her name. Then she rose firmly, and walked steadily to the door.

Just then a man entered within the rail and took her seat. It was her bondsman, Mr. Crane.

XVI

A FRIEND IN NEED

TWO days after Tom had signed the highway contract, Babcock sat in his private office in New York, opening his mail. In the outside room were half a dozen employees — engineers and others — awaiting their instructions.

The fine spring weather had come, and work had been started in every direction, including the second section of the sea wall at the depot, where the divers were preparing the bottom for the layers of concrete. Tom's carts had hauled the stone.

Tucked into the pile of letters heaped before him, Babcock's quick eye caught the corner of a telegram. It read as follows : —

Mother hurt, wants you immediately. Please come.   JENNIE GROGAN.

For an instant he sat motionless, gazing at the yellow slip. Then he sprang to his feet.

Thrusting his unopened correspondence into his pocket, he gave a few hurried instructions to his men and started for the ferry. Once on the boat, he began pacing the deck. "Tom hurt!" he repeated to himself. "Tom hurt? How — when — what could have hurt her?" He had seen her at the sea wall, only three days before, rosy-cheeked, magnificent in health and strength. What had happened? At the St. George landing he jumped into a hack, hurrying the cabman.

Jennie was watching for him at the garden gate. She said her mother was in the sitting-room, and Gran'pop was with her. As they walked up the path she recounted rapidly the events of the past two days.

Tom was on the lounge by the window, under the flowering plants, when Babcock entered. She was apparently asleep. Across her forehead, covering the temples, two narrow bandages bound up her wound. At Babcock's step she opened her eyes, her bruised, discolored face breaking into a smile. Then, noting his evident anxiety, she threw the shawl from her shoulders and sat up.

"No, don't look so. It's nothin'; I'll be all right in a day or two. I've been hurted before, but not so bad as this. I wouldn't have troubled ye, but Mr. Crane has gone West. It was kind and friendly o' ye to come ; I knew ye would."

Babcock nodded to Pop, and sank into a chair. The shock of her appearance had completely unnerved him.

" Jennie has told me about it," he said in a tender, sympathetic tone. " Who was mean enough to serve you in this way, Tom ?" He called her Tom now, as the others did.

" Well, I won't say now. It may have been the horse, but I hardly think it, for I saw a face. All I remember clear is a-layin' me hand on the mare's back. When I come to I was flat on the lounge. They had fixed me up, and Dr. Mason had gone off. Only the thick hood saved me. Carl and Cully searched the place, but nothin' could be found. Cully says he heard somebody a-runnin' on the other side of the fence, but ye can't tell. Nobody keeps their heads in times like that."

" Have you been in bed ever since ?" Babcock asked.

" In bed ! God rest ye ! I was down to the board meetin' two hours after, wid Mr. Crane, and signed the contract. Jennie and all of 'em would n't have it, and cried and went on, but I braved 'em all. I knew I had to go if I died for

177

it. Mr. Crane had his buggy, so I did n't have to walk. The stairs was the worst. Once inside, I was all right. I only had to sign, an' come out again ; it did n't take a minute. Mr. Crane stayed and fixed the bonds wid the trustees, an' I come home wid Carl and Jennie." Then, turning to her father, she said, "Gran'-pop, will ye and Jennie go into the kitchen for a while ? I 've some private business wid Mr. Babcock."

When they were gone her whole manner changed. She buried her face for a moment in the pillow, covering her cheek with her hands ; then, turning to Babcock, she said, —

"Now, me friend, will ye lock the door ?"

For some minutes she looked out of the window, through the curtains and nasturtiums, then, in a low, broken voice, she said, —

"I 'm in great trouble. Will ye help me ?"

"Help you, Tom ? You know I will, and with anything I 've got. What is it ?" he said earnestly, regaining his chair and drawing it closer.

"Has no one iver told ye about me Tom ?" she asked, looking at him from under her eyebrows.

"No ; except that he was hurt or — or — out of his mind, maybe, and you could n't bring him home."

" An' ye have heared nothin' more ?"

" No," said Babcock, wondering at her anxious manner.

" Ye know that since he went away I 've
done the work meself, standin' out as he would
have done in the cold an' wet an' workin' for
the children wid nobody to help me but these
two hands."

Babcock nodded. He knew how true it was.

" Ye 've wondered many a time, maybe, that
I niver brought him home an' had him round
wid me other poor cripple, Patsy — them two
togither." Her voice fell almost to a whisper.

" Or ye thought, maybe, it was mean and
cruel in me that I kep' him a burden on the
State, when I was able to care for him meself.
Well, ye 'll think so no more."

Babcock began to see now why he had been
sent for. His heart went out to her all the more.

" Tom, is your husband dead ?" he asked,
with a quiver in his voice.

She never took her eyes from his face. Few
people were ever tender with her ; they never
seemed to think she needed it. She read this
man's sincerity and sympathy in his eyes ;
then she answered slowly, —

" He is, Mr. Babcock."

" When did he die ? Was it last night, Tom?"

"Listen to me fust, an' then I 'll tell ye. Ye must know that when me Tom was hurted, seven years ago, we had a small place, an' only three horses, and them warn't paid for ; an' we had the haulin' at the brewery, an' that was about all we did have. When Tom had been sick a month — it was the time the bucket fell an' broke his rib — the new contract at the brewery was let for the year, an' Schwartz give it to us, a-thinkin' that Tom 'd be round ag'in, an' niver carin', so 's his work was done, an' I doin' it, me bein' big an' strong, as I always was. Me Tom got worse an' worse, an' I saw him a-failin', an' one day Dr. Mason stopped an' said if I brought him to Bellevue Hospital, where he had just been appointed, he 'd fix up his rib so he could breathe easier, and maybe he 'd get well. Well, I hung on an' on, thinkin' he 'd get better, — poor fellow, he did n't want to go, — but one night, about dark, I took the Big Gray an' put him to the cart, an' bedded it down wid straw ; an' I wrapped me Tom up in two blankits an' carried him downstairs in me own arms, an' driv slow to the ferry."

She hesitated for a moment, leaned her bruised head on her hand, and then went on.

"When I got to Bellevue, over by the river, it was near ten o'clock at night. Nobody stopped

me or iver looked into me bundle of straw where
me poor boy lay ; an' I rung the bell, an' they
came out, an' got him up into the ward, an'
laid him on the bed. Dr. Mason was on night
duty, an' come an' looked at him, an' said I
must come over the next day ; an' I kissed me
poor Tom an' left him tucked in, promisin' to
be back early in the mornin'. I had got only as
far as the gate on the street whin one of the
men came a-runnin' after me. I thought he had
fainted, and ran back as fast as I could, but
when I got me arms under him again — he was
dead."

"And all this seven years ago, Tom ?" said
Babcock in astonishment, sinking back in his
chair.

Tom bowed her head. The tears were trick-
ling through her fingers and falling on the coarse
shawl.

"Yis ; seven years ago this June." She
paused for a moment, as if the scene was passing before her in every detail, and then went
on : "Whin I come home I niver said a word
to anybody but Jennie. I 've niver told Pop
yit. Nobody else would have cared ; we was
strangers here. The next mornin' I took Jennie, — she was a child then, — an' we wint
over to the city, an' I got what money I had,

an' the doctors helped, an' we buried him; nobody but just us two, Jennie an' me, walkin' behint the wagon, his poor body in the box. Whin I come home I wanted to die, but I said nothin'. I was afraid Schwartz would take the work away if he knew it was only a woman who was a-doin' it wid no man round, an' so I kep' on; an' whin the neighbors asked about him bein' in a 'sylum an' out of his head, an' a cripple an' all that, God forgive me, I was afraid to tell, and I kept still and let it go at that; an' whin they asked me how he was I'd say he was better, or more comfortable, or easier; an' so he was, thank God! bein' in heaven.''

She roused herself wearily, and wiped her eyes with the back of her hand. Babcock sat motionless.

" Since that I 've kep' the promise to me Tom that I made on me knees beside his bed the night I lifted him in me arms to take him downstairs,—that I 'd keep his name clean, and do by it as he would hev done himself, an' bring up the children, an' hold the roof over their heads. An' now they say I dar' n't be called by Tom's name, nor sign it neither, an' they 're a-goin' to take me contract away for puttin' his name at the bottom of it, just as I 've put it on

ivery other bit o' paper I 've touched ink to
these seven years since he left me."

"Why, Tom, this is nonsense. Who says
so?" said Babcock earnestly, glad of any
change of feeling to break the current of her
thoughts.

"Dan McGaw an' Rowan says so."

"What 's McGaw got to do with it? He 's
out of the fight."

"Oh, ye don't know some men, Mr. Babcock. McGaw 'll never stop fightin' while I
live. Maybe I ought n't tell ye, — I 've niver
told anybody, — but whin my Tom lay sick upstairs, McGaw come in one night, an' his own
wife half dead with a blow he had given her,
an' sat down in this very room, — it was our
kitchen then, — an' he says, ' If your man don't
git well, ye 'll be broke.' An' I says to him,
' Dan McGaw, if I live twelve months, Tom
Grogan 'll be a richer man than he is now.' I
was a-sittin' right here when I said it, wid a rag
carpet on this floor, an' hardly any furniture in
the room. He said more things, an' tried to
make love to me, and I let drive and threw
him out of me kitchen. Then all me trouble
wid him began ; he 's done everything to beat
me since, and now maybe, after all, he 'll
down me. It all come up yisterday through

McGaw meetin' Dr. Mason an' askin' him about me Tom; an' whin the doctor told him Tom was dead seven years, McGaw runs to Justice Rowan wid the story, an' now they say I can't sign a dead man's name. Judge Bowker has the papers, an' it's all to be settled to-morrow."

"But they can't take your contract away," said Babcock indignantly, "no matter what Rowan says."

"Oh, it's not that — it's not that. That's not what hurts me. I can git another contract. That's not what breaks me heart. But if they take me Tom's *name* from me, an' say I can't be Tom Grogan any more; it's like robbin' me of my life. When I work on the docks I allus brace myself an' say, 'I'm doing just what Tom did many a day for me.' When I sign his name to me checks an' papers, — the name I've loved an' that I've worked for, the name I've kep' clean for him — me Tom that loved me, an' never lied or was mean — me Tom that I promised, an' — an'" —

All the woman in her overcame her now. Sinking to her knees, she threw her arms and head on the lounge, and burst into tears.

Babcock rested his head on his hand, and looked on in silence. Here was something, it

seemed to him, too sacred for him to touch
even with his sympathy.

"Tom," he said, when she grew more quiet,
his whole heart going out to her, "what do
you want me to do?"

"I don't know that ye can do anything," she
answered in a quivering voice, lifting her head,
her eyes still wet. "Perhaps nobody can. But
I thought maybe ye'd go wid me to Judge
Bowker in the mornin'. Rowan an' all of 'em 'll
be there, an' I'm no match for these lawyers.
Perhaps ye'd speak to the judge for me."

Babcock held out his hand.

"I knew ye would, an' I thank ye," she
moaned, drying her eyes. "Now unlock the
door, an' let 'em in. They worry so! Gran'pop
hasn't slep' a night since I was hurted, an'
Jennie goes round cryin' all the time, sayin'
they'll be a-killin' me next."

Then, rising to her feet, she called out in
a cheery voice, as Babcock opened the door,
"Come in, Jennie; come in, Gran'pop. It's
all over, child. Mr. Babcock's a-going wid me
in the mornin'. Niver fear; we'll down 'em
all yit."

XVII

A DANIEL COME TO JUDGMENT

WHEN Judge Bowker entered his office adjoining the village bank, Justice Rowan had already arrived. So had McGaw, Dempsey, Crimmins, Quigg, the president of the board, and one or two of the trustees. The judge had sent for McGaw and the president, and they had notified the others.

McGaw sat next to Dempsey. His extreme nervousness of a few days ago — starting almost at the sound of his own footstep — had given place to a certain air of bravado, now that everybody in the village believed the horse had kicked Tom.

Babcock and Tom were by the window, she listless and weary, he alert and watchful for the slightest point in her favor. She had on her brown dress, washed clean of the blood stains, and the silk hood, which better concealed the bruises. All her old fire and energy were gone. It was not from the shock of her wound, — her splendid constitution was fast

186

healing that, — but from this deeper hurt, this last thrust of McGaw's, which seemed to have broken her indomitable spirit.

Babcock, although he did not betray his misgivings, was greatly worried over the outcome of McGaw's latest scheme. He wished in his secret heart that Tom had signed her own name to the contract. He was afraid so punctilious a man as the judge might decide against her. He had never seen him; he only knew that no other judge in his district had so great a reputation for technical rulings.

When the judge entered — a small, grayhaired, keen-eyed man in a black suit, with gold spectacles, spotless linen, and clean-shaven face — Babcock's fears were confirmed. This man, he felt, would be legally exact, no matter who suffered by his decision.

Rowan opened the case, the judge listening attentively, looking over his glasses. Rowan recounted the details of the advertisement, the opening of the bids, the award of the contract, the signing of "Thomas Grogan" in the presence of the full board, and the discovery by his "honored client that no such man existed, had not existed for years, and did not now exist."

"Dead, your Honor" — throwing out his

chest impressively, his voice swelling — "dead in his grave these siven years, this *Mr*. Thomas Grogan ; and yet this woman has the bald and impudent effrontery to " —

"That will do, Mr. Rowan."

Police justices — justices like Rowan — did not count much with Judge Bowker, and then he never permitted any one to abuse a woman in his presence.

"The point you make is that Mrs. Grogan had no right to sign her name to a contract made out in the name of her dead husband ? "

"I do, your Honor," said Rowan, resuming his seat.

"Why did you sign it ? " asked Judge Bowker, turning to Tom.

She looked at Babcock. He nodded assent, and then she answered, —

"I allus signed it so since he left me."

There was a pleading, tender pathos in her words that startled Babcock. He could hardly believe the voice to be Tom's.

The judge looked at her with a quick, penetrating glance, which broadened into an expression of kindly interest when he read her entire honesty in her face. Then he turned to the president of the board.

"When you awarded this contract, whom

did you expect to do the work, Mrs. Grogan or her husband ? ''

'' Mrs. Grogan, of course. She has done her own work for years,'' answered the president.

The judge tapped the arm of his chair with his pencil. The taps could be heard all over the room. Most men kept quiet in Bowker's presence, even men like Rowan. For some moments his Honor bent over the desk and carefully examined the signed contract spread out before him ; then he pushed it back, and glanced about the room.

'' Is Mr. Crane, the bondsman, present ? ''

'' Mr. Crane has gone West, sir,'' said Babcock, rising. '' I represent Mrs. Grogan in this matter.''

'' Did Mr. Crane sign this bond knowing that Mrs. Grogan would haul the stone ? ''

'' He did ; and I can add that all her checks, receipts, and correspondence are signed in the same way, and have been for years. She is known everywhere as Tom Grogan. She has never had any other name — in her business.''

'' Who else objects to this award ? '' remarked the judge calmly.

Rowan sprang to his feet. The judge looked at him.

"Please sit down, Justice Rowan. I said 'who *else.*' I have heard you." He knew Rowan.

Dempsey jumped from his chair.

"I'm opposed to it, yer Honor, an' so is all me fri'nds here. This woman has been invited into the Union, and treats us as if we was dogs. She"—

"Are you a bidder for this work?" asked the judge.

"No, sir; but the Union has rights, and"—

"Please take your seat; only bidders can be heard now."

"But who's to stand up for the rights of the laborin' man if"—

"You can, if you choose; but not here. This is a question of evidence."

"Who's Bowker anyhow?" said Dempsey behind his hand to Quigg. "Ridin' 'round in his carriage and chokin' off free speech!"

After some moments of thought the judge turned to the president of the board, and said in a measured, deliberate voice,—

"This signature, in my opinion, is a proper one. No fraud is charged, and under the testimony none was intended. The law gives Mrs. Grogan the right to use any title she chooses in conducting her business,—her husband's

190

name or any other. The contract must stand as it is.''

Here the judge arose and entered his private office, shutting the door behind him.

Tom had listened with eyes dilating, every nerve in her body at highest tension. Her contempt for Rowan in his abuse of her ; her anger against Dempsey at his insults ; her gratitude to Babcock as he stood up to defend her; her fears for the outcome, as she listened to the calm, judicial voice of the judge, — each producing a different sensation of heat and cold, — were all forgotten in the wild rush of joy that surged through her as the judge's words fell upon her ear. She shed no tears, as other women might have done. Every fibre of her being seemed to be turned to steel. She was herself again — she, Tom Grogan ! — firm on her own feet, with her big arms ready to obey her and her head as clear as a bell, master of herself, master of her rights, master of everything about her. And above all, master of the dear name of her Tom, that nothing could take from her now — not even the law !

With this tightening of her will power there quivered through her a sense of her own wrongs — the wrongs she had endured for years, the wrongs that had so nearly wrecked her life.

Then, forgetting the office, the still solemnity of the place — even Babcock — she walked straight up to McGaw, blocking his exit to the street door.

"Dan McGaw, there's a word I've got for ye before ye l'ave this place, an' I'm a-going to say it to ye now before ivery man in this room."

McGaw shrank back in alarm.

"You an' I have known each other since the time I nursed yer wife when yer boy Jack was born, an' helped her through when she was near dyin' from a kick ye give her. Ye began yer dirty work on me one night when me Tom lay sick, an' I threw ye out o' me kitchen; an' since that time ye've" —

"Here! I ain't a-goin' ter stand here an' listen ter yer. Git out o' me way, or I'll" —

Tom stepped closer, her eyes flashing, every word ringing clear.

"Stand still, an' hear what I've got to say to ye, or I'll go into that room and make a statement to the judge that 'll put ye where ye won't move for years. There was enough light for me to see. Look at this!" drawing back her hood, and showing the bandaged scar.

McGaw seemed to shrivel up; the crowd stood still in amazement.

"I thought ye would. Now, I'll go on. Since that night in me kitchen ye've tried to ruin me in ivery other way ye could. Ye've set these dead beats Crimmins and Quigg on to me to coax away me men; ye've stirred up the Union; ye burned me stable" —

"Ye lie! It's a tramp did it," snarled Mc-Gaw.

"Ye better keep still till I get through, Dan McGaw. I've got the can that helt the ker'-sene, an' I know where yer boy Billy bought it, an' who set him up to it," she added, looking straight at Crimmins. "He might 'a' been a dacent boy but for him." Crimmins turned pale and bit his lip.

The situation became intense. Even the judge, who had come out of his private room at the attack, listened eagerly.

"Ye've been a sneak an' a coward to serve a woman so who never harmed ye. Now I give ye fair warnin', an' I want two or three other men in this room to listen; if this don't stop, ye'll all be behint bars where ye belong. — I mean you, too, Mr. Dempsey. As for you, Dan McGaw, if it war n't for yer wife Kate, who's a dacent woman, ye'd go *to-day*. Now, one thing more, an' I'll let ye go. I've bought yer chattel mortgage of Mr. Crane that's past due,

193

an' I can do wid it as I pl'ase. You 'll send to me in the mornin' two of yer horses to take the places of those ye burned up, an' if they 're not in my stable by siven o'clock I 'll be round yer way 'bout nine with the sheriff."

Once outside in the sunlight, she became herself again. The outburst had cleared her soul like a thunder-clap. She felt as free as air. The secret that had weighed her down for years was off her mind. What she had whispered to her own heart she could now proclaim from the housetops. Even the law protected her.

Babcock walked beside her, silent and grave. She seemed to him like some Joan with flaming sword.

When they reached the road that led to her own house, her eyes fell upon Jennie and Carl. They had walked down behind them, and were waiting under the trees.

"There 's one thing more ye can do for me, my friend," she said, turning to Babcock. "All the old things Tom an' I did togither I can do by meself; but it 's new things like Carl an' Jennie that trouble me, — the new things I can't ask him about. Do ye see them two yonder ? Am I free to do for 'em as I would ? No ; ye need n't answer. I see it in yer face.

Come here, child ; I want ye. Give me yer hand.''

For an instant she stood looking into their faces, her eyes brimming. Then she took Jennie's hand, slipped it into Carl's, and laying her big, strong palm over the two, said slowly, —

"Now go home, both o' ye, to the house that 'll shelter ye, pl'ase God, as long as ye live."

Before the highway work was finished, McGaw was dead and Billy and Crimmins in Sing-Sing. The label on the empty can, Quigg's volunteered testimony, and Judge Bowker's charge, convinced the jury. Quigg had quarrelled with Crimmins and the committee, and took that way of getting even.

When Tom heard the news, she left her teams standing in the road and went straight to McGaw's house. His widow sat on a broken chair in an almost empty room.

"Don't cry, Katy," said Tom, — bending over her. "I 'm sorry for Billy. Seems to me, ye 've had a lot o' trouble since Dan was drowned. It was not all Billy's fault. It was Crimmins that put him up to it. But ye 've one thing left, — and that 's yer boy

Jack. Let me take him, I'll make a man of
him.''

Jack is still with her. Tom says he is the
best man in her gang.

THE END

www.ingramcontent.com/pod-product-compliance
Lightning Source LLC
Chambersburg PA
CBHW031422250626
47155CB00004B/1586